Full Disclosure

By Mary Wine

Her boyfriend is back...and that's a major problem. Antonia isn't ready to face the one man who shakes up her world...

Antonia doesn't need to look at forbidden fruit. The taste still clings to her lips, haunting her with just how good she and Danton had been together...

...Right up until he informed her that he had to get married because he was going to be a father. That just made it worse. Inside him was a man worth dreaming about, even if she knew it was in vain.

Danton always double-checked his facts. It was a habit that kept him alive during missions that should have killed him. His impromptu wedding was no exception. There wasn't going to be any consummation of the vows until he had a paternity test. But doing the right thing had cost him the one woman he loved.

Until the test came back negative. Now there is nothing that will stop him from coming back with the prize he'd been forced to abandon three months ago. Toni was going to be his, right after she got the full disclosure on his hasty wedding and the blunt fact that he loved her.

Warning, this title contains the following: explicit sex, graphic language and bondage bedroom games with toys.

Spontaneous

By Karen Erickson

Hot summer nights make people do crazy things.

Sophie Kincaid doesn't want to be attracted to her boss but she is. Sick and tired of being used by men, she's sworn them off. But her hot and now slightly drunk boss just became too hard to resist.

His girlfriend dumped him and now Ian Grey is drowning his sorrows in alcohol, something he never does. Flirting with Sophie the sexy bartender inspires him to do even more things he'd never consider. Like have hot sex with her in the storage room.

They can't deny their attraction for each other but Sophie's afraid she doesn't measure up. And what does Ian want from her anyway? She'll have a naked good time figuring it out...

Warning this title contains the following: Hot, steamy, explicit sex and graphic language.

Bad Moon Rising

By Elle Kennedy

Does a full moon really cause naughty behavior?

Hailey Burke has heard that full moons cause people to behave in strange ways, but she never thought it would apply to her until the night she winds up in bed with a man she doesn't even like. So she'd had a temporary loss of sanity when she slept with Zack Creighton, the womanizing photographer. Big deal. Doesn't mean she's going to do it again, right?

Wrong.

Unfortunately, Zack has something else in store for Hailey. He's liked the sassy redhead from the moment he met her, but he can't get the stubborn woman to let go of the misconceptions she's formed about him. Sure, he's played the field, but Zack is no womanizer, and he has no intention of leaving things at one night. Once he's had a taste of Hailey, he wants another. And he's determined to convince her that he's not the bad boy she's always thought.

Warning, this title contains the following: explicit sex, graphic language

One Night on a Balcony
By Samantha Lucas

One hot summer night and a scorching balcony interlude light the fuse of hidden attraction between neighbors Jill Reed and Cole Adams.

Jill Reed has spent her entire life denying her sexuality, but living next door to Cole Adams the past few months has made it near impossible.

Cole is fresh off his third divorce and considers himself a one-man relationship train wreck. He purposefully keeps his lust for Jill in check because, after all, she's the kind of woman a man keeps.

Jill and Cole have been denying their bone-deep attraction for months, but one night on a balcony, passions ignite, an adventure starts and everything is about to change—forever.

Warning, this title contains the following: explicit sex, sex in a public place, graphic language.

Hot Summer Nights

A Samhain Publishing, Ltd. publication.

Samhain Publishing, Ltd.
577 Mulberry Street, Suite 1520
Macon, GA 31201
www.samhainpublishing.com

Hot Summer Nights
Print ISBN: 978-1-59998-779-8
Full Disclosure Copyright © 2008 by Mary Wine
Spontaneous Copyright © 2008 by Karen Erickson
Bad Moon Rising Copyright © 2008 by Elle Kennedy
One Night on a Balcony Copyright © 2008 by Samantha Lucas

Editing by Sasha Knight
Cover by Scott Carpenter

Full Disclosure, 1-59998-574-8
First Samhain Publishing, Ltd. electronic publication: June 2007
Spontaneous, 1-59998-591-8
First Samhain Publishing, Ltd. electronic publication: August 2007
Bad Moon Rising, 1-59998-576-4
First Samhain Publishing, Ltd. electronic publication: June 2007
One Night on a Balcony, 1-59998-586-1
First Samhain Publishing, Ltd. electronic publication: July 2007
First Samhain Publishing, Ltd. print publication: June 2008

Contents

Full Disclosure

Mary Wine

Chapter One

"This is mean, cruel and I think prosecutable."

Brenda only laughed as she offered up a glass mug as a peace offering. Antonia wasn't willing to settle so easily.

Okay, if it was a *really* good ale in that frosted mug, she might be willing to negotiate, but only if they were talking stout ale, on tap and brewed by a company that wasn't located in the United States.

And chilled. The August night was blistering. Even her slip-on sandals made her feet sweat. The sun had set hours ago but the air was still warm, promising another night of eighty-plus-degree weather.

"Stop whining, Toni. You used to love this place." Brenda batted her eyelashes as she pressed the mug into Toni's hand. "You need a drink and a little fun. So stuff it, sister, and chill out."

Antonia sent her friend a sour expression before closing her hand around the mug. Her fingers tingled from the tiny ice crystals clinging to the glass as she lifted it to her nose. A little mutter of delight rose from her lips as she took a sniff of the brew. There was nothing quite like a true ale.

So what if she had odd habits? The rest of the Saturday-night crowd could drown in their beer, she wanted ale. Not that drinking her problems away was any sort of favorite pastime.

But enjoying a cold mug would be a pleasant moment in between the bitter hours of heartbreak. The overhead fan at least moved the air around. A thin draft of air conditioning blew past, but the bar-slash-restaurant was too crowded for any machine to keep pace with the weather and the crush of people. Besides, the power had been going on and off for most of the week as residents flipped on the air conditioning in order to fend off the heat wave. It was Southern California at its best.

She fingered the menu but the only thing that appealed was the ice cream. With a little shrug of her bare shoulders, she laced her fingers around her mug. Who needed food when you had good English ale?

"You need to get laid."

Toni choked on her ale and slammed it down onto the table. "Brenda!"

Brenda rolled her eyes and smirked. "Well, you do and..." She held up a finger to keep Toni from blurting out another response. "And...you know it too. Getting dumped by one guy does not put you out of the game. Sexual tension turns even the sweetest gal into a bitch. Just admit you're in the grip of a storm of hormones. That way, you can keep your friends. You shouldn't let one guy spoil the whole relationship thing. Find someone else." Brenda's eyes closed to slits as she pointed a long, blood red polished nail at her. "Just don't let him turn you into a bitch. You know, bitter, pitiful."

"Depends on the guy." Toni wasn't impressed with her response. It sounded lame, even to her ears.

Brenda pushed the ale back towards Toni before giving a delicate wave of her hand. "There are plenty of fish in the sea."

Toni lifted her mug to her lips to hide her frustration. Fish? Yeah, sure, but she wasn't interested in normal guys. That was the main problem with tasting a real man. Now anything short of full-grown men had sort of lost all of their attraction. Getting laid wasn't worth it if she wasn't going to take a mature man home. Quality instead of quantity. She shook her head as she looked around the bar. So what if she wasn't ready to get back on the horse? The bright side was that tomorrow morning she wouldn't be worried about contracting AIDS. Besides, in this heat, body-to-body contact wasn't the most appealing thing she could envision.

"Oh my...my...my." Brenda grabbed Toni's wrist as she stared across the bar to the game side of the place. All ten of the pool tables were in play and Brenda pointed at one of them. "I think your luck just changed."

Toni followed the line of Brenda's finger and hissed as she found who was on the other side of the bar. Her luck certainly had changed, but not for the better. Danton Reeves straightened up as the men watching his game nodded approval at him. Her gaze slid over his frame because she just couldn't help but look at what she was still craving. Danton was one hundred percent lean man. His shoulders were packed with hard muscle, and his body tapered down to a tight abdomen. Looking good was one thing, but Danton knew exactly how to use his body. His control and focus made sex something so incredibly intense. She was still abstaining, because she hadn't found anyone who was his equal, despite the fact that he'd tossed her over for another woman. No one sent a shiver down to her toes or drew her attention quite the same way. It wasn't even a choice sometimes, her gaze just moved to his without any forethought. It was completely frustrating but too vivid to shake off.

So she was a complete idiot. That didn't alter the fact that Danton made her jumpy, just by being in the same room. He turned his head and caught her staring at him. His lips moved slightly before Toni jerked her gaze away from him. Just because she hadn't gotten past their break up, didn't mean she needed to share that rather stupid feminine response with him. Another thing the man did disgustingly well was read her emotions right off her face.

"Oh come on, Toni. Don't freeze up on the guy."

Toni glared at her friend. "Excuse me, but I'm not going to play a doormat for him."

Brenda licked her lower lip. "I would, at least for one wild night."

"Have fun. I won't wait up for you."

Brenda snickered at Toni's sarcasm and crossed her eyes at her before standing up. "Fine, you win. Enjoy being a martyr."

Toni narrowed her eyes, but her effort was wasted as Brenda moved across the floor with a slow sway of her hips towards a group of her friends. Her loose sundress slithered around her thin body.

Toni wasn't a martyr.

She was selective. Captain of her own destiny.

Her gaze moved back towards Danton and disappointment shot through her. He was gone. Vanished, just like he had three months ago. If Brenda hadn't seen the man as well, Toni would be questioning her own eyes. It was an honest fact that she thought about him too much. He pranced through her dreams in spite of numerous self-inflicted lectures to forget him. Falling in love was a high-risk thing because sometimes you ended up being alone with the emotion. In spite of months of lonely nights, her fickle mind refused to let his memory go.

Her pager went off, and she grabbed it gratefully. She recognized the local sheriff's station's number and was already walking towards the back of the bar before she reached for her cell phone to call in. A social worker had to be on call twenty-four hours a day, seven days a week but tonight she was grateful for a reason to slip out of the bar early. She was going to let her job be the cover for her quick exit. It wasn't grand, but it would serve as an escape route. The only part she didn't like was the fact that she'd have to put on a blazer to make herself presentable in the professional work world. Anything with sleeves made her frown; a suit jacket was cause for profanity.

She moved towards the back door, looking for a quiet-enough spot to hear the desk sergeant. People were crowded into every square inch of the place in an effort to soak up the air conditioning. Pushing through the back door, she flipped open her cell phone. The night air was warmer than it had been inside but the door closed off the music. She punched in the first digit of the sheriff's station's number.

She never got to the second. The phone shut as her hand was gripped in a much larger one. She opened her mouth to let out a scream, but a hard palm covered her lips as she was pressed up against the wall behind her. A moment of terror gripped her, sending her heart into a frantic pace that made her lungs draw deeper breaths. The scent filling her senses was recognized instantly. She shivered as Danton's solid body held her captive with the door behind her. Her nipples tightened into twin points that stabbed into his chest. It was that quick and beyond her control. There was no thought, only reaction. Her temper exploded as their eyes met in the dark. Only Danton did this to her. One touch, one stroke, and her body transformed into a traitor. It just made it worse that the arousal came in the wake of him scaring her half to death. Men were inherently jerks. It was a cruel twist of fate that she wasn't a lesbian and therefore immune to males.

"Hello, Toni. I've missed you."

He leaned completely against her and she gasped as the clear proof of his statement made itself known. His cock was hard. The muscles of her belly quivered as he pressed against her, while he watched her intently. She was helpless in his hold, but true to his nature, Danton never tightened that grip enough to hurt her. The amount of weight he used to secure her bordered on suffocating but he managed to keep it from becoming painful.

That was one of the things that frustrated her the most; his control. In everything he did, the man was a study in focus. Even the most intimate things became soul-meshing experiences under his tight handling.

The man could make her scream.

Chapter Two

"Let me go. I need to call in before I lose my job." Toni shut her mouth because her voice was too needy. A corner of Danton's mouth curved. The damn man always knew when he was getting to her. Just like a shark smelled blood and moved in for a kill.

"No you don't. I arranged the page."

"Bull—" Toni shut her mouth once again before she finished her comment. If anyone could pull a string at the local sheriff's department, Danton was that person. The man had friends in every form of law enforcement, civilian and military. "Fine, get off me. It's too hot for body hugs, in case you hadn't noticed."

Another lame excuse but at least she wasn't reaching to complain about the weather.

He leaned closer instead. "I enjoy hugging you, Toni."

A shiver raced through her body and his eyes flashed in response to the telltale motion. Her lower lip was suddenly too dry, and she licked it before logical thought rose up to warn her against the impulse. Danton's gaze dropped instantly to her mouth as his chest rumbled with a low growl. That was the other thing about him that made it vital to escape. He responded to her like oil tossed onto an open flame. They mirrored each other's passion back and forth until it became a firestorm beyond any kind of control. Only the idea of getting as close as possible remained in her thoughts. No barriers, no distance, only deep and primitive contact.

"We need to talk, Toni." Danton stepped away from her and her nipples ached with disappointment. That lament traveled down to her clit as she watched his face tighten with the same unanswered need. His gaze swept down, lingering on her chest. The thin tank-top dress wasn't any help in hiding the twin points now that they were hard.

Well, at least she wasn't alone. His jeans were bulging at the front too. It was small comfort but she'd take what she could get. Misery loved company after all.

Danton showed her a half grin before offering her a helmet. She licked her lower lip again as she looked past him to the motorcycle parked right next to the back door. Oh Lord...she remembered that machine. As powerful as its owner, the thing was sleek and lean. Climbing onto the back of it would ensure a victory for Danton over her protesting better judgment. There was no way she could wrap her arms around him and hold onto any idea of keeping the man out of her bed. Hell, she wouldn't need a bed, just the hard body of the master of the mean machine. She could feel the first drops of fluid easing down the inside of her passage as she stared at the helmet.

Temptation was a mean, cold-hearted bitch tonight.

"I don't think that's a good idea. In fact, I'm sure it's a bad idea." She sounded defeated, but there was no help for that. She craved another wild night, in spite of knowing it would end with her right back where she'd been...lonely and still in love with forbidden fruit. Not to mention that she'd be wearing the title of home wrecker. Danton was a married man, she had to keep that in mind. If he'd cheat on a wife, he'd double-cross her too. All that did was make her heart hurt even more. She wanted to keep her sterling ideal of him, even if she couldn't have him.

"Wrong." He stepped closer once more, crowding her against the door. She had to tip her head back to stare at him. Something flickered in his gaze that looked like desperation, and that confused her. Danton had never struck her as needy before. He was always the pillar of strength.

"I don't do new-husband panic attacks, Danton." Toni moved away from the door, and his gaze followed her as she placed a few feet of space between them. Disappointment flared through her, but she savored the feeling as a reminder of what she tended to receive from Danton. Hard, painful lessons needed to be remembered or you ended up repeating the class. Losing him once was enough for her.

"I'm sorry you're having trouble settling in with your new wife, but I'm not going to feed you. My bed is off limits now that you're married. You'll have to adjust to home life. Go back to your wife for both our sakes. I'm not a home wrecker." *I'll get my own man...somehow, someway.* "I'm going home, you should do the same."

She turned her back on him and fumbled in her purse for her car keys. Getting home was a necessity; she didn't need to display her addiction for him where he could see it. Some things were better left buried along with a broken heart. It was like a raw wound that refused to begin closing because she kept fussing with the bandage.

"Sure, Toni, I'll do that." His voice was rich but coated in a soft amusement that drew her attention back towards him. Danton swung one leg over his bike and pulled his helmet on as he watched her. "Thanks for the advice." He turned the engine over and rode smoothly off into the flow of traffic.

A warning bell was going off somewhere in the back of her head but she couldn't quite put her finger on exactly why. Only a sneaking suspicion that Danton didn't ever give up so simply. That, or she just didn't want him to be finished with her so quick.

That was idiotic, to say the least.

All right, now she was being stupid, but lying to herself wouldn't solve anything. Being so happy at the idea of him looking for her tonight was going to land her in a pot of trouble. There were a lot of things that she thought about him, but "cheating dog" had never been one of them. Danton had always kept his word and told her straight what his opinion was. His touch left a sour taste in her mouth tonight because she had never once pictured him as a lying husband.

Damn it. The least he could have done was let her keep her image of him. Losing that was another twist of the knife. The dull pain hit her hard as two tears eased from her eyes.

Chapter Three

"When are you going to learn to lock your windows down?"

Toni shrieked as she hit the light switch and her keys clattered onto the floor of her entryway. Danton glared at her from across the room. His face was set into a deep frown as he tossed a look at her living-room window. The curtain was pushed aside, telling her exactly how he'd gotten into her home.

"That's stupid, Toni, really dumb. I didn't secure this house to have you let laziness allow someone to break in. You know how to lock it down and how important it is." Anger laced his voice as he glared at her. "I thought you were safe."

Heat burned across her face as she recognized her own failing. Oh yeah, she'd messed up. Danton had spent two days installing window locks and outfitting her little house with security equipment. She shook her head as she switched back to him being in her house without her permission. Danton had an annoying habit of tailoring conversations to support his opinion. Even when he was misbehaving, he turned the tables to make it look like he was doing you a favor by pointing out your weaknesses.

No way was she admitting any kind of mistake to the man tonight. Even if she should have locked her windows before heading out. It wasn't his job to educate her.

"Excuse me, but you're the one breaking in right now. I'm not one of your Special Forces men who will benefit from your training exercises. Get out."

He crossed his arms over his chest and smiled at her. It wasn't a pleasant expression though. His lips curled up to show his teeth. "If you're so confident of your position, make me leave."

She flipped her cell phone open and pressed the nine key. A second later, Danton's hand clamped around her wrist. He pulled her arm across his body to his opposite hip. A swift twist of his midsection and her body whipped around his like a damp towel because of his grip on her wrist that pulled her arm taut across his wider body. He let her go and she stumbled to a halt, but without her cell phone. Danton held it up for her furious glance before pushing it into his shirt pocket. The man never wore something simple like a T-shirt. There was always a neat row of buttons down the front of his chest, and pockets; the sort of shirt you expected to see a hiker in. A garment built for utility. Even his jeans were the type with sturdy pockets that buttoned. That was Danton for you; all business, and deadly in the execution of it. Her little dress felt like tissue paper compared to his capable appearance. While she'd dressed to endure the weather, he was outfitted with survival in mind. Comfort was measured by his clothing being just baggy enough for him to move with ease. No skintight jeans for him, his pants had enough fabric in them to allow for moves like the one that had just netted him her cell phone.

Leaving her neatly at the mercy of his goodwill.

A little shiver shook her spine as she recognized how much strength he really had in his body. He had always been careful not to hurt her, even in their most intimate moments. Trust was a double-edged blade because she honestly couldn't evict him on her own. She'd only been bluffing with her cell phone and he'd called it. That left her high and dry with no recourse.

"Damn it, Toni. Don't look at me that way." He made a disgusted sound under his breath before he dug her cell phone out and tossed it across the distance to her. "I told you we need to talk." He watched her catch the little bit of technology. He stared at her for a long moment to see what she'd do with the returned cell phone. A frustrated growl escaped her lips as she stuffed it into her purse. Calling the cops wasn't the answer, in fact, it would only serve to tie her into a knot of tension as she waited for Danton to corner her in some other place. The man didn't know the word "quit" existed in the English language. If he intended for them to have a talk, he'd keep appearing until he was satisfied. The man's tenacity was frustrating but it was also admirable—if you enjoyed satire.

He grunted approval. "Next time, dial it in your pocket so that your unwelcome guest doesn't know what you're doing. You'd have been dead long before the local patrol car made it into your driveway, if that was my intention."

"That's assuming rape isn't on your mind."

A ghost of a grin curved his lips. "Don't make suggestions you don't want me to take interest in. Seducing you sounds like a lot of fun."

Toni hissed at him. Conversations with Danton spiraled out of control faster than paper caught fire. Only tonight, she was the one dealing with the heat boiling up inside her. Her body didn't much care about the details. But she sure didn't need him painting a picture that she'd have to sleep with in her unsatisfied dreams once he went home to his new spouse. "What do you want, Danton?"

His face lost all traces of humor as he moved closer. His feet never made a sound, even on her hardwood floor. Toni fought the urge to wiggle backwards as he kept moving. She had to lift her chin so their gazes locked, but she refused to budge and show him any weakness. That need burned bright enough to keep her in place in spite of his body looming over her. He turned his hand over and stroked one side of her face with the back of it. Sensation rippled down her spine. Her nipples tingled before drawing into tight little nubs. Danton's eyes blazed into hers as that ripple went lower, making her shift as her clit softly throbbed.

"You. I want you back, Toni." His voice was husky with desire.

His opposite hand snaked around her waist. That quickly she was a captive of his stronger body, held against him while his fingers moved around to cup the back of her head. He considered her intently, like he was memorizing her trapped in his embrace. A shudder shook her body as her hands pushed against his chest. It was a feeble excuse for a protest, one she couldn't maintain for very long. Her hands smoothed over his chest, transmitting just how hard the man who held her still was. Heat raced through her veins as she felt her mouth go dry in anticipation of his kiss.

It had been too damn long since he'd kissed her. Right and wrong didn't hold much value as she watched his gaze drop to her mouth. On instinct she licked her lower lip. His eyes followed the tip of her tongue as they narrowed.

"You are so damn sexy. The way you move, even breathe. It turns me on instantly. I haven't had a single night's sleep since we parted without seeing you in my dreams." His mouth blocked out any response she might have made. His hand tightened on the nape of her neck to control her head. Pleasure flooded her starving senses as he pressed her lips apart. He'd been the last man to kiss her and right then, it seemed like she'd been poised for three whole months waiting for this second. A little mutter of delight rose from her throat. Danton didn't rush the kiss. He lingered over the first meeting of their mouths before increasing the pressure by small degrees. He teased her to open her jaw, and the promise of sharing his kiss again was too much.

She wouldn't burn in Hades over just one kiss...right?

The tip of his tongue traced her lower lip. Her lips parted further as he thrust his tongue into her mouth. He stroked her tongue as the kiss became hard and demanding. His body moved until they were flush against each other. The arm holding her back draped lower until his hand cupped one side of her bottom and pressed her hips forward. One thick thigh pressed between hers until he could rub it against her mons. Her clit clamored with appreciation as he stroked it, even through her dress. Danton released his grip on her bottom and she curled her hips back from him only to have him press her right back into solid contact with his thigh. Sensation shot into her pussy, shaking her with a deep pleasure intense enough to steal her breath.

Toni broke off their kiss as she gasped. Danton rubbed her mons again with his knee as his fingers roamed over her bottom, gently squeezing in a purely sexual way. His cock was hard against her ribs, taunting her with just how much she wanted it back inside her.

"You're married." Trying to cling to her sanity, Toni pushed against the body she craved. If she stayed in his embrace, tossing him out was going to slip right out of her mind. She wasn't sure she could face the morning alone after a fresh taste of him.

Danton released her and a twist of pain went through her heart. Toni focused her attention on that evidence of what Danton brought into her world. Pain. They were bad for each other, addictive in a fashion because neither of them was moving on very effectively. Like junkies, they were panting for another taste even though they both knew it couldn't last.

"I won't be married for much longer."

"Excuse me?" Her voice trembled because his words were pure temptation. Her body certainly liked the idea of Danton being back on the list of acceptable men. She wasn't the staunchest member of her congregation, but she drew the line at breaking commandments. Adultery was off limits. She grasped at her rational thinking while trying to keep her mind on the facts that had split them apart and led him to the altar.

"Look, Danton, you two are going to have a baby. You need to go home and iron out whatever sent you here tonight. Kids need a home. I understood your reasons. But I can't have an affair with a deadbeat father. Even you." Looking into his eyes, she soaked up every bit of strength she saw burning there. Plain and simple, she loved him because of the man he was. "Don't tarnish my vision of you by asking me to be your lover. Please."

"It's not my kid." Danton's fists tightened until she heard the knuckles pop, and the raw fury of betrayal flashed in his gaze. For a man like him, dishonesty was the worst of all sins, especially over a child. Locked up in his chest was a heart that loved family. He'd walk through fire for any and all family relations. "Come on, I need some air before I forget all about discussing anything with you and drag you back to your bed."

He wasn't joking. There wasn't a hint of mercy on his face, nothing but the blazing need in his eyes. Her body shouted for her to fling out a denial, just to wave the flag in front of the bull to see if he'd charge her. But it was a cowardly impulse, a way of shoving aside her principles in favor of letting Danton take responsibility for their passionate explosions.

Danton was worth better than that. He deserved a woman who stiffened her spine and gave him that same hard honesty right back. That ground rule fueled their passion because, as lovers, they told each other exactly what they craved. It took them on a journey through desire and need that scorched every inch of her flesh, even touched her heart.

"Sure." Toni reached for a ponytail holder and twisted it around her hair to secure it back. She refused to think about anything else as she opened her closet and found the jacket she couldn't bear to part with. It was dark plum leather, the first gift she'd received from him. The garment represented his growing need to share more than sex with her. He had given her the jacket so she could ride on his motorcycle with him. It was an invitation he'd never extended to another woman.

Only to her.

Even in the anguish of heartbreak, she'd been unable to part with it. Maybe just because she knew his new wife didn't own one.

"You kept it."

Toni shrugged into the jacket and turned to face him. Danton was right in front of her and she jumped. He caught the open front of the riding jacket to hold her in place as he stroked his hands over its smooth surface and the curves of her breasts. Something drew his features tight. It was hard to put a description on the emotion because it was too vulnerable for a man who was as solid as steel.

"Yeah, I kept it."

A flare of passion lit his eyes before he clamped his jaw tight and turned towards the door. He clasped one hand around her wrist, closing his fingers in a grip that was almost too tight. A little ripple of fear raced down her spine as she recognized how helpless she would be leaving on the back of his bike. In a way, she got the idea that he liked knowing she was in his control. There was a part of her that enjoyed it too. A crazy little twist of sensation went through her clit as she anticipated being dependant on him. It was a dark idea, rich with hints of domination and capture. Telling Danton what she liked in bed was intense, but being under his command was decadent.

She shivered as his bike came into view. It was top of the line and customized. Danton pulled his helmet from the seat and swung his leg over the bike. He was the master sitting there strapping his helmet on. A second helmet was attached to the back of the seat and a ripple of anticipation raced down her spine as she recognized the details of a perfectly planned mission with her as the objective.

"What if I didn't have the jacket anymore?"

His teeth reflected moonlight as he grinned at her. "You would have worn mine." All traces of playfulness evaporated as he watched her secure the strap of the helmet. He kicked the support stand up and turned the key. The engine rumbled to life as he jerked his head in invitation.

"Let's go, Toni. If you want your explanation before I get back inside you, get your ass on this bike."

She understood Danton well enough to not take offense at his words. Hell, it excited her to hear how much his control was being tested. There wasn't a sweet-worded compliment that could affect her as deeply. They fed off each other's arousal. He was offering her the choice to settle their mental debate before they appeased their need. It was leave now, or let him get back inside her. It was getting harder to remember just why she was walking away from her condominium with its air conditioning and waiting bed.

Toni swung her leg over the back of the bike and gasped as the vibration of the motor hit her aroused clit. He pussy was already growing wet. By the time they got to wherever Danton wanted to go, she was going to be poised on the edge of desperation. She wrapped her hands around his waist and he took off.

"And may God have mercy on us both." Her words were whisper soft and lost in the engine noise, but no less true.

Chapter Four

Danton clenched his jaw against the wind. He enjoyed the burn of arousal. Toni clung to his body, driving the heat in his cock up another degree. His memory was clear as crystal. When he was deep inside her, she'd whimper and clasp her thighs around his hips. They had explored every position he knew for fucking, but, in the end, there was nothing quite as primitive as pressing her down onto her back so that his chest rubbed against her breasts while he rode her.

He shook off the idea as he tried to regain a measure of control. He'd be back inside her soon, but he owed her an explanation. It didn't matter that someone owed him a hell of a lot more for messing up his life for the past few months. All that fucking mattered was that Toni had kept the riding jacket, proving that she wasn't finished with him either.

She loved him. He knew it, and he was grateful for it. More humbled than he'd ever stinking been in his entire career storming hostile locations around the globe, places that should have swallowed him and spit his lifeless body out onto the ground. Living through eight years of active Special Operations duty dulled compared to being so close to Toni again. Maybe distance did make the heart grow fonder because the last three months had felt endless.

℘℘℘

"It's Hooker's baby."

There was a note of disappointment in his tone, but it was far overshadowed by anger. Danton threw a stone into the water and it skipped across the surface of the lake perfectly before he turned to look at her. He moved in stiff, jerky motions. Energy bled off him like an aroma that was designed to stimulate her appetite.

If that was the case...it was working just fine. Despite the warm night air she felt a chill go down her spine that had nothing to so with the lake nearby. Toni unzipped the jacket now that the motion of the ride wasn't cooling her anymore. The moonlight rippled along the water's surface, setting the scene perfectly for summer lovers.

"Ronda had to have one of those amnio tests done. I requested a paternity one while they were at it."

"She agreed to that?" Toni was shocked. Ronda Valencia had screamed to high heaven that Danton had knocked her up and left her while he went off after Toni. The thing that had torn her life apart was the fact that Danton admitted to sleeping with Ronda before Toni had been ready to begin the physical side of their relationship.

"I didn't ask her permission. She had the test done on base and I needed to know if that was my baby."

"Oh." That explained a lot. Danton wasn't just military, he was Special Forces. If he didn't have a buddy in every office on base, he knew someone who did. That was what he was, the ultimate adapter and survivor. He would get what he needed in any manner necessary. Danton didn't lose. Ever.

"Well, you're still married. I'm sorry, Danton. Maybe she just doesn't know for sure...you know? Some women are more popular than others."

"You mean less discriminating." He stared at her for a long moment. "Is there someone else in your bed, Toni? Since I left it?"

He really didn't have the right to ask when he'd been sleeping with a wife while they'd been apart. Her heart leapt at the opportunity to try and build a bridge back to where they could be together. But it hurt to reopen the door that led to trusting him with her bare feelings. "I wasn't the one who got married."

"Toni..." His voice turned dangerous. Another rock went skipping across the lake before he turned and sprang at her. The impulse to move didn't make it to her feet in time. Danton closed his arms around her and she shivered as she caught the warm scent of his skin. It was like musk, hitting her senses and seeping in to trigger all her hormones. He grasped her jaw and raised her face to his. "I need to know. Has there been anyone else? Tell me, so we can get past it."

Her temper flared up in the face of his demand. "Oh, aren't you arrogant. Get past what? You've been playing house with Ronda."

"I never consummated the marriage. If the kid was mine, I'd have stood by her, but it's not my baby. If something was going to cost me you, I was going to make sure first." There was another flash of harsh emotion in his eyes. Toni stared at his face like a starving person. Danton watched her in return for a moment. "When I confronted her with the test, she admitted that she'd slept with Hooker. The second test came back positive in his favor. Our marriage is being annulled right now because I never screwed her. I haven't been inside any woman since I laid down beside you. When I told you I loved you, it was the honest truth. I've never been in love with a woman other than you." His thumb smoothed her bottom lip. "But I am arrogant." His knee pressed between her thighs once more, and a little moan escaped her mouth as her clit was rubbed. Another wave of need washed through her.

"You've got that part right. You reek of arrogance." She could feel the fluid soaking into her panties as her body heated for his possession. His declaration rung through her head, making thought almost impossible. She'd heard him say he loved her in her dreams so often the moment was almost surreal.

"Just tell me if there was someone else, Toni." His gaze flashed with determination as his thigh moved against her clit again.

The scent of her wet pussy rose between them and it was too damn much to ignore. He was suddenly grateful for the little excuse of a dress she was wearing. It was loose and fell to her knees with nothing more than a string to keep it closed. He growled in approval. "God, I've missed just how receptive your body is." Popping the tie open, he caught the sides of the skirt and pulled it up and over her head.

"Danton..." Her voice was coated in apprehension. He didn't stop, only smoothed his hand down her bare thigh in a motion meant to be gentle. He lifted her right off her feet, and her little beaded Indian-harem shoes slipped off her feet. Her dress fluttered into a puddle, leaving her amazedly at his mercy. The hard bulge of his cock pressed against her hip as Danton stepped towards his bike and sat her on the seat. His body spread her legs wide and her little lace-edged panties weren't any protection.

"There hasn't been anyone since you left." Her breath was husky but rushed as his hand brushed up the center of her slit. Sometimes, hard and rough sex was a relief, but Danton's cock was large and her body was going to be tight from abstinence. His hands froze for a moment in a little telltale reaction to her confession.

And it was a confession, an admission of his remaining hold on her. She had had every reason to move on and hadn't. Tonight, with his warm fingers spread out over her belly, it felt incredibly right to be in his embrace. Pride didn't feed the need clawing at her and it didn't satisfy her desire to be held once passion was fed.

Danton would.

Her body recalled that fact too keenly. Her hips thrust towards his body as her nipples drew into hard points. Blood rushed through her veins, flooding the tiny vessels that ran close to her skin, making the tissue acutely sensitive. She felt each fingertip where they rested on her.

Danton held her chin in a firm grip and raised her face to his. There was the brush of his breath against her wet lower lip before he pressed a soft kiss onto her mouth. His hand slid down the smooth skin covering her belly and onto her mons. He broke the kiss as a deep rumble of male appreciation shook his chest.

"I love your waxed pussy." His fingers slipped over the soft skin and into the top of her slit as she shivered. "But I love this clit even more."

Danton broke off his next comment because it involved women from his past. They didn't belong anywhere near Toni. He indulged the raw possessiveness of that idea. His finger touched her clit, and she quivered against him. The folds of her sex were slick with her arousal, making him groan with need.

His cock was too hard for playing. A fire burned in his gut to get back into her like some primitive claiming ceremony.

But there was one thing he was going to do first. He hooked an arm around her body as he rubbed her clit with a fingertip. Her hands gripped his biceps as she gasped and wiggled against the pressure on that sensitive button at the top of her slit.

"Danton." Her voice was low and husky, completely betraying how much she enjoyed being fingered. She had battled for years with her high sex drive, not really finding any peace until Danton joined her in bed and taught her to embrace her greedy flesh. Her hips curled up, eager for deeper penetration. Pleasure tightened under his touch like a knot being pulled. She dug her fingers into the hard arms holding her, and feeling the steel of his biceps intensified her need to buck her hips towards her lover.

"Come. Right on my finger, Toni."

He pressed harder, and her body convulsed as climax jerked through her. She cried out as she arched away from him and over the bike, her thighs clasping his legs where he stood between her spread ones.

He caught the back of her neck with his hand and angled her head up to look into his face. His jaw was clenched tight, the muscles of his neck corded. His finger slipped down her slit to circle the opening of her pussy.

"We're getting married. Just as soon as I get the final annulment papers."

His voice was harsh. Like a drill sergeant instilling discipline in his newest recruits. But the need coating that deep tone touched her heart. It wasn't something communicated through words very well. They were addicted to each other, the sex and the conflict, but most importantly to the emotion that

sent them into the night where spreading her thighs on a motorbike was not only desired...it was craved.

"I love you, Danton. I never stopped." It was so easy to say, even in the face of months of heartache.

"Don't ever stop."

His hand left her sex as he stepped back slightly. There was the faint sound of his fly opening before he pressed her thighs wider with his body.

"Hold on to me, baby."

She gripped his arms as his cock nudged her slit. Her climax had ensured that there was plenty of fluid to ease his entry into her body. Danton gripped her hips as he thrust forward. A hard groan shook his chest as he forced himself to stop only halfway into her.

"You're tight. So damn tight." He lifted his face and locked gazes with her. "I love you so damn much for not fucking another guy. Shit, you had every right to. But I'm so goddamn glad you didn't."

He pulled free and pressed back deep. His cock stretched her pussy, the passage aching slightly as it took his length again. Sweet pleasure surged through her as he slowly left her before thrusting once more. He made sure to slide his entire cock against her clit without rushing each stroke. The bike vibrated beneath her bottom, forcing her to control her own motions and let Danton take command of their pace or topple the machine. It was pure torment, waiting for his next penetration. He lingered deep inside her pussy for a moment that seemed like an eternity before moving again. She was balanced on the sharp edge of need the entire time. The pleasure shot through her, twisting and tightening as her hips tried to lift towards his steady thrusts.

Danton cussed and his hands gripped her hips as he lost his private battle to control his pace. He nipped the tender skin of her neck with a soft bite before whispering against her ear, "I can't go slow anymore, baby. I need to fuck you like I've been dreaming of." He held her hips in an iron grip while his body drove into hers faster and harder. Their voices mixed as she whimpered and he grunted. Pleasure built under the motion of the hard cock rocking her. He snarled softly before she felt the first spurt of his seed hit her womb. She jerked as she realized he hadn't donned a condom tonight. It was the only time he'd ever fucked her bare. Her pussy contracted around his length in a frantic attempt to milk his seed deep into her belly. The pleasure that whipped through her was blinding. It shot up her spine and slammed into her brain. Her vision went dark as she panted to supply her racing heart with enough oxygen. Danton held her through the storm as her body twitched and bucked towards him.

She collapsed and he hugged her against his chest. The fabric of his clothing irritated her face as she shuddered with the last ripples of sensation.

"I'm sorry, Toni. That was rough." His hand smoothed over her skin but she didn't hear any lament in his voice. It was pure male smugness.

Wiggling against his hold, she pushed at his chest. "It's too hot tonight."

His teeth flashed in the moonlight. "Come on, the lake will cool us off."

He lifted her off the seat of the bike and waited as she found her shoes. Her dress was flung over his shoulder and he clasped her hand without giving her dress back.

"Give me my dress, Danton."

A soft chuckle was his reply as he tugged her forward. "No one's around. Hear the birds? They'd be silent if anyone was nearby." He turned his head and his gaze swept her from head to toe. "I like you just like this. You should wear that outfit more often. I love it."

He guided her along a dirt trail. It ended on a small dock. Her dress landed on the sanded planks. He unlaced his boots and sat them next to her dress. A giggle got caught in her throat as they stood there naked. It was naughty but oddly perfect; standing near the water cooled the air down a few degrees.

"Come on, Toni, the lake is great tonight." A huge splash sent water sprinkling over her bare skin as Danton cannonballed himself into the smooth surface of the lake. She laughed as the water hit her. It was a delicious combination of sin and sensation. She hadn't been skinny-dipping since she was eight years old and her schoolyard friend had dared her to do it.

"You're a bad influence, Danton."

He shook water out of his eyes and grinned at her. "Come here, Toni."

She sat and dangled her feet in the lake, kicking some more water at his face. He was treading water using slow backwards strokes of his powerful arms, the muscles standing out in the moonlight.

"What made you think the baby wasn't yours?" She needed to know, because it was almost surreal to have him back in her life so simply. It felt like a dream-spun fantasy and the alarm clock was going to shatter her bliss any second now.

He blew out a long breath. "Gut feeling more than anything. That and I only had intercourse with her one time. We used protection as well."

"That's all it takes, you know." The warning lost a lot of its impact as Toni considered the fact that they hadn't used protection fifteen minutes ago. She wasn't in any position to judge Ronda.

His gaze dropped down her nude torso as a half grin lifted his lips.

"Yeah, I know." Husky arrogance was back in his tone. His gaze centered on her belly for a long moment. "I didn't bring any condoms with me."

Toni felt her face turn red. Sure, she was still using birth-control pills but they'd always doubled up before. It should have pissed her off; instead it hit her as a symbol of his devotion to their relationship. That and there was something exciting about hearing him tell her that he had planned to try and make their new start as permanent as possible.

"I wouldn't have left you for anything else, Toni."

She sighed as her emotions rolled and tried to send tears down her cheeks. It horrified her to feel her composure teetering so easily. His gaze studied her intently. But his cheek twitched in response too.

"You can be damn sure I wasn't going to consummate that marriage until I saw a paternity test. Now or after the birth there was no way I was giving you up without proof positive."

"Well, you sure didn't share that information with me." She hated the hurt lacing her voice but there was a part of her that needed to know he understood how deep his leaving had cut her.

"It would have left you in limbo." His voice was firm in his belief in his choice. Toni shook her head because she knew better than to argue with that tone. Danton wouldn't back off a decision. Not without an elephant leaning on him anyway.

"I know you still love me, Toni. Love like that doesn't die. What I'm back to find out is whether or not you can trust me." The water splashed as his strokes became harder, betraying his emotions. "Love isn't worth spit without trust. A marriage isn't worth a dime without it either."

"I know." And the fact that he did made her heart fill up to bursting. It was a silly emotion, one better suited to teen magazines and soap operas but tears tumbled from her eyes and they were ones born from love. Danton watched her face, smiling as he witnessed the overflow of emotion. She kicked another round of water at him as she pushed her lower lip out in a pout. "Why do you have to read my expressions so well?"

"Because I love you. If I was more interested in my cock, I'd never notice what bothered you."

She rolled her eyes. He curled one finger in her direction. "Ready to join me?"

She jumped in and giggled as the water swallowed her up. It was still warm from the blazing sun, but coupled with the darkness, it was now just right. Midnight was easing on them as a breeze kicked up, rustling the dry leaves of the surrounding trees. The wind picked up a tiny amount of water, making the air cool as it touched her face.

Two hands captured her hips as Danton pulled her towards him. The water was only chest-high on him and he was standing on the bottom of the lake.

"Much better. This heat wave is testing my patience. We may have to spend every night for the rest of the month up here because I need to be pressed against you." He leaned down to nip the side of her neck once more.

"Poor baby." Her teasing mood died as his cock brushed against her leg. It was hard again and she shivered as she realized that he'd be a lot longer before climaxing this time. His hands smoothed down over her hips to tease the center of her bottom. He fingered the opening to her ass for a moment before gripping each thigh and spreading her legs around his hips.

"Hold on to me, honey."

Her hands clasped his neck as he thrust up into her again. It was a smooth penetration that satisfied the hunger flickering through her body. With him filling her once again, she wasn't sure she had ever been sated.

"Now lock your legs around my waist."

She did it but frowned at him. "I forgot how much you enjoy giving orders."

His hands grasped her bottom as he pulled free and then thrust back up into her. Pleasure rose from the friction of his motions, making her shiver.

He growled softly and bit her earlobe. "I haven't forgotten how much you enjoy being mastered. We'll have to play some more games, honey."

She gasped as he moved again, pressing deep as the water splashed around them. If he came again, he'd have enough endurance to drive her insane when they got back to her place.

But he wasn't in the mood to climax. His hips thrust hard against hers without increasing the speed. Pleasure tightened in her belly with the motion of his hips while the water swished around them. Her fingers dug into his shoulders as her body tumbled into another climax, this one deeper but smoother. He thrust a few last times before simply holding her, clasped tightly to his body with his cock still hard inside her. His eyes reflected the moonlight as he studied her face before placing a warm kiss to her neck, licking over the bite he'd left on the sensitive skin.

"Let's go to bed." His voice was husky and hungry again. But he lifted her off his length and climbed out of the water. He offered her a hand as the moonlight turned him silver. A hard shiver shook her as she reached for it.

For Danton, the night was only beginning.

Chapter Five

The ride back to her house felt twice as long as it had when they left. Maybe it was the vibration of the bike against her clit or the scent of his skin, Toni didn't know. She was drowning in sensory overload, but quite content to let it drag her down into a pool of sensations where she might lose track of where her body ended and his began. Her pussy felt empty and her clit throbbed for more attention. The shake of the bike wasn't enough to make her climax; instead, it kept her clit jiggling just enough to ensure she was impatient to get to her driveway.

That was another detail about Danton that had haunted her since their separation. His ability to build her hunger throughout the night, fanning the flames. It was never one round of sex and then turn the late-night sports channel on. He was the perfect companion because his appetite matched hers. They were like a pair of mirrors aimed at one another.

The night was a cloak that helped them slip away from reality. Danton parked his bike in a dark shadow cast by her garage. One large hand captured hers, and his fingers closed around her hand. He led her around the back of her condo. Her nipples tingled, drawing tight with anticipation as she handed over her set of keys without a word. Heat snaked its way up her pussy making her eager to chuck her clothing the second that door sealed out the rest of the planet. Her skin wanted to be free so that she could feel him pressing against her from head to toe. She wanted to feel every touch and not through the layers of their clothing.

"Let's shower."

That was for her sake. Toni knew it as she followed Danton into the bathroom. He flipped the water on without any light. Moonlight streamed in through the upper portion of her bathroom window. That was enough light for him. His night vision was another one of those things that made him dangerous. He really was a deadly predator, complete with keen senses that allowed him to blend into his environment and surface when he wanted to make a kill.

Or claim a mate.

Her thighs were sticky with his seed and she shivered as she caught him watching her undress. The moonlight splashed over his bare body, making her stare at the perfection of his nude frame. Every muscle was cut and molded. Dark hair covered his chest, running down across his belly. Her nipples tingled again as she remembered exactly what it felt like to have his crisp hair rubbing against her breasts when he pressed her down onto her back for a hard round of fucking. His cock thrust up from his belly, erect and swollen. Reaching out, she clasped it with one hand, letting her fingers move around it.

She suddenly wanted to shift the power balance. Apply her own brand of demand and have Danton shivering because of her actions. Lowering herself to her knees, she licked the slit on the head of his cock. His breath rasped through his teeth on a harsh note as she opened her mouth and took the entire crown inside. Closing her hands around the remaining length, she worked her fingers up and down his cock as she took as much as possible into her mouth.

"*Christ,* Toni!" The glass wall of her shower rattled as his back knocked against it.

She wanted to smile, but kept her mouth in place, teasing the little slit with her tongue. Danton clasped her head in one large hand as his hips began to thrust towards her mouth. Smoothing one hand all the way to the base of his staff, she gently handled the sacs hanging there. Danton snarled softly.

"Go on and play, honey. Because I'll be looking forward to my turn."

Her clit throbbed at the idea. Turning her head, she applied more attention to his cock, listening for a response. A sharp rasp of his breath was her reward as she stroked her fingers back up his erection. His hips kept thrusting as she sucked more of his length inside her mouth. His breath was harsh and grew labored before he grasped her neck to pull her away from him. Solid determination tightened his features when she looked up at his face. The shower was still spraying out cool water. The air conditioner was finally getting the upper hand against the heat now that the night moved towards the early-morning hours. Her skin was cooling off, and pressing up against his warmer male body felt inviting.

Danton held a hand out to her.

"Come on back here, baby. I'm not going to come again for a long time." His voice was thick and gruff with promise. A surge of confidence rose inside her as she felt the tremor shaking his huge body because of her actions. But she shivered too as she recognized his husky tone. It was a warning that he was in the mood to fuck. It wasn't a need that was going to be fed quickly.

He grasped her hand and pulled her off her knees. They didn't have a lot of room, but Danton wasn't interested in any separation. He stood behind her as the water flowed over them both. His hand cupped her breasts as he applied some soap to the soft globes. He rolled her tight nipples between his thumb and forefinger as his hard cock thrust against her bottom. He bent his knees slightly to lower his hips to fit between her thighs. Her pussy was still wet, and the water eased his path as well. His hands smoothed a soapy trail over her chest to her belly as he clasped her waist and entered her.

"Do you hurt?"

His cock was completely lodged inside her body again. Her pussy smarted from being stretched around his girth, but the pain wasn't strong and it snaked through her, fueling a wild enjoyment of being filled.

"Not bad enough to stop."

Danton chuckled. He leaned over her shoulder and bit the lobe of her ear. "Spread your feet." It was easy to obey on the wet tile. Another shudder worked its way down her spine as she complied. With him in back of her she was left waiting for his next move. Danton caught her wrists and placed her hands flat against the tile wall. She leaned over to do it and he pulled her hips so that her bottom rose slightly towards him.

"Now that's a perfect submissive position."

"Submissive, like hell!"

Toni jerked back into a standing position and his length slipped from her body. Her pussy complained about the loss as she tried to turn and face Danton. He captured her wrists instead and molded his body over her back, effectively imprisoning her with his larger, stronger frame. He bent her back over, pressing her hands onto the tile as his cock teased her wet slit. Her clit throbbed as his erection lightly grazed it. Pleasure snaked up from the contact, whetting her appetite for more.

"I like the idea of you being submissive." His breath hit her ear as he pulled his hips away from her and then slid his length through her slit, taunting her with its swollen hardness without penetrating her. "I like it a whole lot." He bit her ear and stroked through her open sex again. This time, she whimpered as her clit begged for a firmer connection. The tiny sound was like blood in the water and Danton caught its scent instantly.

"Don't move or your Master won't be pleased."

"Master, my ass."

He tsked at her defiant tone, but released her wrists and straightened up. Toni bit into her lower lip as she debated her options. A little moan left her throat as she recognized Danton's intention. The man was in the mood to drive her insane.

"Yes, Master does like your ass. Thank you for offering it."

Toni gasped as his hands smoothed over her raised bottom. There was the slick glide of soap over each side of her fanny before Danton separated the cheeks and cleaned between them. The shower was still pumping out water and it carried the soap down her legs while Danton fingered her back entrance.

"Still have your plug?"

She shivered with anticipation. Danton was the only man who had ever touched her ass. "Umm...yes." She mumbled the response, embarrassed to say such a personal thing out loud.

A hard smack landed on her butt and she yelped.

"You will answer in a full voice."

"Yes! I have it." Her face burned as she heard her words echo inside the shower stall.

"You have what?" He fingered her back opening, inserting one fingertip. Pleasure shot up into her belly as she lifted her bottom towards the touch without hesitation. Her memory demanded that she comply with his game, because the pleasure would be ultra intense if she yielded to his command.

"I have my butt plug."

His finger withdrew from her, and a whimper marked its departure. Another smack landed on her raised ass; it was harder, but the pain went straight into her clit, making her moan as need clawed at her to do whatever it took to gain connection with his cock again.

"Do not yell at your Master." One thick finger thrust into her pussy. Her hips lifted for the penetration as her pussy tried to contract around that one digit. Danton leaned down over her back, stroking her spine until he was pressed along her back with his breath teasing her ear. He gently raked the skin on her neck with his teeth, sending sensation down her nerve endings. The finger inside her pussy began to move in and out as she gasped with the pleasure. He stroked her slit until he reached her clit, lingering for a long moment on the sensitive bud.

"Your Master can deliver pleasure but only if he is pleased with your submission."

Her entire body shuddered as the idea of playing submissive exploded in her brain. Danton felt the reaction and applied his teeth to her ear in another soft bite. "Interesting idea isn't it, Toni? Complete submission. I think we should try it."

He rubbed her clit as she whined and tried to press down onto his hand. Danton stood and drew his finger from her spread folds. The water hit her unprotected back, sending a new set of signals through her overstimulated flesh.

"Master wants you to dry off. You will lay your plug and the lubricant on the bed before getting onto your hands and knees in the center of the bed to wait for your Master. You may not watch for me. You will lower your head until your face is in the bedding, to prove your submission."

"You are such an arrogant bastard." Every inch of her body was poised in anticipation but that didn't mean that her pride liked the details.

"And you love it." He smacked her ass and the water popped loudly. "Go on, Toni. Wait for me with your ass in the air."

She cast him a fuming look as she stomped out of the bathroom. But Danton was more interested in the way her nipples remained contracted into tight little points. Toni might not like his handling technique but her body enjoyed it. It was a harsh side of sex that he could only explore with her. She struck a missing chord in him that he hadn't noticed the lack of until moments like this when he wondered if she'd be waiting on her bed for him. Excitement nipped along his cock, tightening his balls as he rubbed a towel over his skin.

Toni might not like the idea completely but they were going to explore it because this relationship was for the long haul.

There was a part of him that needed her to comply just because he'd asked it of her. It would deepen his confidence in their relationship because only a woman who loved him would put up with his arrogance.

But he would make sure to see that it was worth her time.

Chapter Six

It was stupid. Something from a porno film gone bizarre. Educated women didn't play closet games that included calling their lovers "Master". At least not women who held decent-paying jobs and didn't need to be classified as "kept".

But it excited her. The idea refused to budge from her brain as she used a towel to dry her skin. Anal intercourse was something she had only ever worked up the courage to try with Danton. Challenging the taboo fit with his dark persona, feeding some wild side of her own personality that had never found an outlet before. It was like having the decent, respectable boyfriend who you could show off to your parents but also play in the dark hours with the bad boy you knew your mother wouldn't approve of.

The combination was mesmerizing, taunting her with the taste of more than just sweet seduction. An entire array of flavors sat waiting for her to sample them, even if a few of them might sting.

Danton was poised on the edge of need, battling his inner beast. That was something he enjoyed. The burn of challenge was addictive, it was what got him through military Special Operations training programs designed to crack even the strongest man. To succeed, you had to get in touch with that primitive side of your nature. A man needed to learn just how much leash to allow the animal.

Part of that was wondering if Toni would choose him just the way he was, with all the rough edges still on. It wasn't that he needed a submissive female; what he craved was a woman who could adjust to his moods. A woman who wasn't going to shatter emotionally if he was too abrupt, or freak out if he reacted to an unexpected threat.

But more importantly, he wanted to know if Toni could play in bed with him the way they had before. Could she roll with the punches and take a chance on him again? He'd never lived his life in the shallow end of the pool. He wanted it all, needed to taste foreign dishes simply to experience the flavor.

Tonight he wanted to sample walking into her bedroom and seeing her poised on her bed...waiting for him. His cock twitched at the idea as he forced himself to remain in the bathroom. Anticipation tried to drive his heart rate up and Danton controlled it with iron willpower. He gritted his teeth against the burn moving through his balls. He knew one thing for sure, her submission was the sort of flavor that would leave a mark in his memory until his dying day. It would set his entire body on a slow burn just like a habanera pepper did when you ate it. The heat lasted for hours, moving through your entire body and forcing you to sweat. He grinned because that was exactly what Toni did to him. One taste and he lingered in her grip for days.

Seeing Toni's ass waiting for him could do that. Hell yeah, it could. He tightened his hands into fists as he listened for a sound from her bed, telling him that she was ready for his mastering to proceed.

Chapter Seven

She was excited.

Toni pulled the small drawer in her nightstand open and looked at her meager collection of adult toys as heat blazed through her. Danton had gifted all of them to her, and she'd been ignoring them since their split-up because they reminded her of his presence in her bed. Easing her own sexual tension while sleeping alone hadn't appealed because each naughty adult plaything only reminded her of how much she'd enjoyed the man who wielded them so expertly on her body.

Another shiver shook her as she reached for the butt plug. It was a large one, and she picked up the tube of gel that went with it. Her gaze lingered on the full-sized dildo still in the drawer, but she closed it and moved towards her bed with only the plug. She didn't want a toy in her pussy tonight; she craved Danton's cock. Maybe that was blunt, but it was true. Sex toys could be enjoyable, but there was a part of her that needed to be fucked by the real thing. A toy didn't satisfy the same way for her.

A crazy twist of excitement went through her as she placed the plug and lubricant on the bedspread. Her ears picked up every sound in the room as she listened for his approach. She turned around and assumed the position he'd requested, and her clit throbbed with anticipation. With her knees placed apart on the bed, the fold of her slit opened slightly. She actually felt the air brushing the wet surface of her tender flesh. Her vision was useless as her face was placed against the cool cotton of the comforter covering the bed, and the rest of her senses began working overtime in response.

The skin covering her bottom tingled as it waited for the first touch from her lover. Each second felt like an hour as she listened for a footfall or some other sound. That was part of the game though, the anticipation. Danton could move silently and was often in the room before she knew he was there. Her heart raced as she gripped the comforter with her hands, trying to control the urge to look behind her. Excitement held her on edge, growing with every breath she took until she gave into the urge to peek behind her. Toni looked at the doorway and gasped as her gaze touched on her lover. His attention was centered on her displayed bottom, hunger drawing his face taut.

"Sweet submission. I could get used to walking into the room and seeing your body waiting for me." He stroked each side of her bottom with a firm hand, slowly massaging her cheeks before trailing his fingers through her slit. "Have you used the plug without me?"

"No." She shivered as she felt the touch of the lubricant against her back opening. Danton teased the puckered area with a single finger as he spread more of the slick gel inside her ass.

He chuckled softly and she squirmed as she battled against the urge to move away from his touch. No other man had ever tempted her to sample anal penetration; somehow, with Danton it wasn't forbidden territory. He was temptation, pure and simple, so everything they did was coated in that dark excitement. It was as decadent as rich chocolate.

"Do you know why, Toni?" He pressed the first inch of the plug into her bottom as he spoke. She whimpered as sensation shot into her clit from the penetration. "You need to have a man who you respect mounting you." He pulled the plug free and pressed it back into her bottom. "There's no feminine equality about it. Deep inside your brain is a female who enjoys the fact that I hold you down and fuck you."

He worked the plug in and out, twisting it with each thrust. Her brain wrapped around his words, and she moaned as need began to build to an unbearable level. One touch on her clit and she would come. It was that acute. A low growl rose from her throat and it didn't even sound human. She heard a harsh intake of breath from Danton before the plug was pressed back into her bottom. It smarted, but the pain transformed into pleasure as she muttered the only word her mind could form. "More.

"Oh yes." Her hips twitched, trying to move towards him, desperate for friction against her clit. "Fuck me. Please."

A hard smack landed on her bottom instead. Toni snarled as she pushed up off the bed. Danton caught her and flipped her over onto her back. She didn't remain in the helpless position but curled up off the mattress to slap his hard chest. She needed an outlet for all the sensation. He growled as her hands connected with his firm flesh. He grasped her hips, pulling her hard against his body before rolling onto his back. She ended up on top of him as he held onto her hips.

"Master says for you to fuck him."

"About time you asked for something I agree with," she snarled at him as she braced her knees on the bed on either side of his lean hips. Lifting her body up, she felt the head of his erection nudge her wet slit.

"Ride my cock." His eyes were bright with demand and need.

He pushed her down onto his length as he bucked beneath her. With the plug in her bottom, her pussy was tight and she shivered as his cock filled her. He watched his rigid flesh disappear into her body before looking up at her face.

"Ride me, Toni."

"Yes, Master." She braced her hands on his shoulders and gripped his hips with her thighs. She shivered as she rose off him and then let gravity help push her back onto his hard length. Climax began to twist through her as she lifted and pushed back down quickly, impatient to release the need he'd built up inside her.

"That's it, baby, take what you want."

Danton gritted his teeth as he watched Toni fuck him. Her face was tight as she panted. She rode him fast, her pussy making little wet sounds while she fucked him. She yelled as she came, and her hips pressed down, grinding against his cock. Her body jerked and quivered as she cried. Danton surged up off the bed, flipping her onto her back the second her pussy began to contract around his length. Control vanished as he hammered his cock into her spread body. Her moans mixed with his snarls while the bed rocked. It was a hard possession as he let the animal inside him claim exactly what he wanted from her.

Toni refused to think. It was impossible to do anything but feel. Danton growled a moment before his seed flooded her once again. This time, he pushed her down into the mattress, holding her as he came. It was difficult to fill her lungs because his body trapped hers so completely, but a second climax rippled through her as his cock pressed and ground against her clit. She sobbed as she struggled to breathe and her fingers caught the tremor moving though his body. Perfection really was simple. People messed up their own lives by trying to think out things that should be allowed to come naturally. She'd never intended to fall in love with Danton, in fact, her logical mind warned her away from him but love didn't listen. It showed up and no amount of thinking made it understandable.

Love didn't make sense. But it felt amazing.

ℰᗪᏟℬ

"Come on, Toni, we need another shower."

This time he washed her. Bathed her as gently as he would a baby. Toni stood under the warm water, unable to think beyond the way his hands felt on her skin. He removed the plug carefully, taking care to do it slowly. She was sore, but so satisfied it was a battle to keep her eyes open. Danton dried her off like a prized sports car before he clasped her hand and took her back to bed.

He pulled her into his embrace, even trapping her legs with his as he tucked a sheet around them. He caught her chin and raised her face to meet his eyes. In the dark room, only moonlight shimmered off them both.

"I'm sorry I didn't disclose all the facts to you, Toni, but I thought you'd be able to move on easier if I didn't tell you I had doubts about the baby's paternity." He stroked her face gently as his lips curved into a smile. There was such intensity in his mood; tears stung her eyes as she witnessed it. No one had ever been so devoted to her before. It communicated far more than any three little words could ever do. Saying he loved her was one thing, right now she felt cherished.

"I know you had to be sure, you're not a jerk. That's the real reason I didn't date anyone else. You're a hard act to follow."

"You're impossible." His voice was husky with emotion now. "Tell me you'll marry me."

Toni giggled instead. "Arrogant man. You ask me... Will you marry me?"

"Yes, I will."

Toni punched him in response. But since she was lying against his shoulder, the blow didn't have any real force behind it. She pouted at him. "Loving you is going to a bag of surprises, isn't it?"

"Yes, ma'am." His face went serious as he stroked a hand over her hip. "Will you have my baby, Toni? Leave those birth-control pills in the cabinet and just take a chance with me? No waiting, there will never be a perfect time. Life isn't that way. I didn't care for how it felt to get split apart. Maybe it's the kick in the ass I needed. I want commitment, right now, no waiting, let's just jump. As long as we have each other, I don't give a damn how cold the water in the river is, we'll adapt."

"There's no other man on this earth who I'd agree to do that with but you."

They might plan for a decade and never find the perfect time to begin a family. Maybe Danton had the right idea, jump in and swim. He wouldn't let them drown. Love gave her the kind of faith to believe in him like that; that unshakable foundation that a couple could build a life on.

"I would be honored to become your wife, but I have one condition."

"And that is?"

Smoothing her fingers across his forearm, Toni smiled at the contrast between her slim fingers and his harder, male ones. "We stay friends too."

Her voice coated his ears, filling in all the nicks and bruises the last few months had left on him. Danton listened to her breathing as it slowed and deepened. For ten years, he'd lived his life out of a duffle bag. Tonight, he was going to hang it up in a home.

"Yes, Ma'am."

Their home. It was perfect because it was built on love.

About the Author

To learn more about Mary Wine, please visit www.marywine.com. Send an email to Mary at Talk2MaryWine@hotmail.com.

Look for these titles by *Mary Wine*

Now Available:

Evolution's Embers
Let Me Love You
Still Mine

Spontaneous

Karen Erickson

Dedication

To my family for their never-ending support.

Chapter One

Sophie stopped short when she saw *him* sitting at the bar.

Ian Grey never, ever sat at the bar. Rumor had it he flat out didn't drink. *Ever.* She'd worked at the bar in the Royal Plaza Hotel in San Francisco for the last six months and she couldn't remember him staying in the room for more than ten minutes, tops. Rather unfortunate considering what delicious eye candy he made.

With her new resolve though, she didn't pay attention to eye candy. Or at least she tried not to. Delicious men were dangerous, and Sophie Kincaid had had enough of dangerous delicious men to last her a lifetime.

So what was the general manager of the Royal Plaza doing there, she wondered as she slowly walked towards the bar counter. And with a sweating drink in front of him?

"...so she broke up with me. After five years of my life in a relationship with a woman I thought I was going to marry, she dumps me. Just like that."

Sophie's ears perked up at that statement. Perfect Ian Grey got dumped by his equally perfect girlfriend? She hadn't heard that particular rumor yet.

Chuck, the bar manager, nodded in commiseration and Ian knocked back the rest of his drink. "Tough breaks, man."

"I was gonna marry that woman. I'd planned on buying her a ring for Christmas." Ian shook his head and stared into his glass.

Sophie shuffled her feet and gnawed on her lip. It was almost six o'clock, time for her to start her shift with Chuck for the busy Friday summer night. She needed to get behind the counter, needed to get to work, but she didn't want to butt in on what sounded like a rather personal conversation.

"Hey, Sophie."

She glanced up and found Chuck smiling at her, a look on his face that read *rescue me*. She started towards the bar, sauntered really, deciding to work it for the efficient, sexy man who ran the entire hotel with a straightforward intensity she'd never witnessed before.

After all, he just broke up with his girlfriend. A little wiggle in her ass and a thrust of her chest might be what he needed to make him feel better.

"Chuck." She bent to put her purse in a cabinet beneath the bar and turned to find Ian Grey's dark blue gaze settled in the exact spot where her ass had just been. "Mr. Grey. What brings you here tonight?"

His gaze lifted, met hers and he smiled. A sensual smile that revealed straight white teeth and curved his firm lips invitingly. Those lips tempted her to lean forward and touch his mouth with her fingers.

And then maybe follow up with her tongue.

"Hello, Sophie. And please, call me Ian."

Hearing her name on his lips did something to her. Made her shiver from the inside out, made her want to know what his voice sounded like when he breathed her name in her ear. Right before he buried himself deep inside her.

Sophie shook her head and started moving down the bar, wiping the already clean counter with a damp cloth. She needed to stop thinking like that. Doing so had gotten her in way too much trouble in the past. Too many men, too many who used her, treated her like shit, even forgot her name. One who even smacked her around, though she'd wised up and left him relatively fast.

The last one had not only stolen her heart, but he'd also stolen all of her money and her credit. It devastated her so much she lost her previous job and her apartment. She'd had to move back in with her mom for a few months to get herself back on her feet both mentally and physically.

When the job listing for a bartender at the Royal Plaza Hotel appeared in the *Chronicle*, she immediately applied. Okay, yeah, she knew it was kind of trashy that her past bartending experience had been at the Wily Fox, a popular strip joint in the heart of the San Francisco Tenderloin district. She had made a lot of money at that place in tips, just for flashing a little bit of cleavage. She also learned a lot and became a skilled bartender. She'd even been in line to be lead bartender until Marty screwed it all up. Marty, the boyfriend bouncer who helped her lose her job as well as his own.

God, what a jerk he'd been. And he hadn't even been that good in bed, despite his boasting around the club. No, he'd turned out to be a muscle-bound jerk with bulging biceps and a pencil dick.

Not that skilled with it, either.

The phone rang and Chuck gestured towards it. "You'll take care of the boss while I go answer it?"

Sophie gave him a firm nod, feeling the warm and intense gaze of Ian on her backside. "Of course, don't worry about it."

Chuck left them alone, and she was suddenly afraid to turn around, afraid to face the far-too-handsome man who sat before her. But she did so, their gazes locking, and the air immediately filled with an unseen crackling energy. Fingers of heat seemed to radiate off him and towards her, beckoning her to him. Luring her in.

She'd always been a sucker for a handsome man with dark hair and a sexy smile.

"Can I get you another?" She tilted her head towards his empty glass, fascinated at the sight of his fingers twirling it around, his blunt fingertips tracing the rim. She could imagine those fingers touching her, tracing along her body. Delicate yet firm, his touch would arouse her to climax with ease.

He stopped twirling the glass and pushed it towards her. "Why not?"

"What are you having?" She placed the glass in the sink and pulled out a clean one.

"Jack and Coke."

"Coming right up."

Ian watched her fix his drink, his gaze steady on her. "You like working at the hotel?"

"Oh, yes." She set the fresh drink in front of him. "I love it here. Everyone seems to love working here."

"I'm glad to hear it." He sipped from his glass. "Do you work here full time? Forgive me for not remembering."

She smiled. She'd forgive him for just about anything if he kept looking at her with those sexy blue eyes and intense expression. "Yes, I'm the only other full-time bartender besides Chuck."

"So is this what you want to do with your life? Or is this a temporary thing while you're working towards something else?"

Sophie shrugged, uncomfortable with his questions. No one ever asked her what she was doing with her life. She just—lived. "To be honest, I haven't figured that out yet."

"You haven't?" He looked incredulous. "If you don't mind my asking, how old are you?"

"Twenty-eight." And feeling more uncomfortable by the second.

"Huh. I can't imagine going through life not knowing what was going to happen next."

Thank goodness, a couple sat down at the opposite end of the counter and she walked over to take their order, away from Ian's intense scrutiny. She supposed that was part of the attraction for her, his intensity, his single-minded focus. She could only imagine that intensity focused solely on her while he touched her. Stripped her of all her clothing. Pounded himself deep inside her, his eyes locked with hers as his cock filled her.

Crap, all of this intensity was getting to her, breaking her even. She didn't need this, didn't need to feel so serious, so worked up over a man. After her vow to herself a few months ago, she knew she couldn't allow herself to fall hard for someone who would only end up breaking her heart. Considering he recently broke up with his girlfriend and he just happened to be her boss, Ian would most definitely end up breaking her heart.

Sophie served the couple their drinks, then went back to check on him, deciding it was time to lighten things up.

Ian watched her approach, appreciating the shift of her hips in her tight black miniskirt, the swell of her breasts beneath the fitted sleeveless shirt. He could see her bra through the thin white fabric of the shirt. He could make out the white lace cups that hugged her rounded curves too. God help him

67

but the idea of unbuttoning her shirt, revealing her lace-covered breasts to his gaze turned him on, made his dick hard.

Hell, everything about the sexy bartender made his dick hard. He hadn't been this hard since...

He didn't know when. Certainly not in the last few years with Nadia. Their sex life had gotten so stale he could count on a roll in the sheets once a week, usually on a Saturday, at approximately ten o'clock. His life had turned boring in a blink of an eye. And he desperately wanted to do something about it.

"Can I ask you a personal question?"

He glanced up, found Sophie watching him with an amused gleam in her blue-green eyes, her full lips pursed.

He shrugged. "Depends on how personal you want to get." Shit, did that come out sounding sexual? Because he didn't mean for it to sound sexual.

Okay, maybe he did mean it to just a little bit.

"It's not too personal, don't worry. I just wanted to know something." She leaned across the bar, resting her arms on it. A daring look shone in her eyes. "Have you ever done anything spontaneous?"

Ian sat up straighter. What kind of question was that? Of course he'd never done anything spontaneous. He planned his life down to the letter. He'd worked hard his entire life to get what he had, and barely had time to even think about being spontaneous, let alone actually *do* anything spontaneous.

Yet another thing to add to the list of what made him feel really, really boring.

"I can be spontaneous." He knew he sounded defensive, but he didn't care. "I just never have time."

She shook her head, a tiny smile curving her sexy lips. "That last sentence says it all. No one makes time to be spontaneous—you just are." She shifted, her forearms still resting on the counter. He swore she did it on purpose, to give him a better view of her delectable cleavage. He couldn't help himself, he tipped his head and looked down her shirt and actually saw the white lacy cups of her bra. *Fuck.*

Her breasts looked plump and full, and he imagined them filling his hands. Pink nipples hard and begging to be touched and sucked. He could almost hear her little gasps and sighs when he put his mouth on her...

"Haven't you ever done something crazy? Without any thought? Like buy five-hundred-dollar sheets even though you're broke, or go on an unplanned vacation without any luggage? Or maybe have a hot one-night stand with someone you're attracted to but know you'll never see again?" Sophie paused, her eyes meeting his. "Have you ever done anything like that, Ian?"

This was not the kind of conversation he should be having with an employee, even though she wasn't under him directly. Still, it was completely inappropriate. And he was all about appropriate. "Have *you* done any of those things?"

She smirked. The sight of it made him want to kiss it right off her face. "Guess which ones. I've done two out of the three."

He needed to walk out of the bar right now. Really. Things were happening that he hadn't planned. First of all, there was the drinking. He was so unused to consuming alcohol he could feel the buzz coming on. Hell, it was already on. Second, the flirtatious conversation with a woman he'd secretly lusted for since she walked onto the hotel premises and applied for a job. Third, the fact that he was now a single man and contemplating making a play for his lusty sex object. All of this equaled...spontaneous actions. Well, hell.

"Okay." He sighed, dragging his index finger through the water ring his sweating glass left on the counter. "I'm pretty sure you've paid five hundred dollars for sheets when you were broke."

"Yep." Sophie nodded, a giant grin on her face. "They are the softest sheets I've ever slept on. Well worth the money."

His head was suddenly filled with images of soft cotton sheets sliding against naked bodies, long legs tangling with his. Blonde hair spilled across a plump pillow, blue-green eyes cloudy with passion staring into his...

Then he remembered the last time he had sex with Nadia, and how crappy it had been. How disconnected she had seemed. He didn't know what was worse, remembering how bad his last sexual encounter was or torturing himself with an overactive imagination about a sexual encounter he was never going to experience. At least, that's what he told himself.

Her expression was naughty, as if she knew what he was thinking and he swore she pressed her breasts together with her arms to make deeper cleavage. "So tell me, what's your other guess?"

"The one-night stand?" Just saying it made his forehead break out in a faint sweat. His imagination filled with thoughts of having a one-night stand with her. Doing whatever he wanted with her, to her. Letting her do whatever she wanted with him, to him.

Sophie laughed triumphantly and slapped her hands down on the counter directly in front of him. "Wrong! Wish I would've made a bet with you, I could've made some easy money."

"So you've gone on vacation without any luggage?" That surprised him. Who the hell went on vacation and didn't take anything with them?

She stood a little straighter, his cleavage view now gone. He didn't know whether to sigh in relief or cry with disappointment. He had a distinct feeling he was drunker than he realized.

"I was involved with this guy, a really rich guy. One Friday afternoon he called me and asked, 'You want to go to the Caribbean?' I laughed and said, 'Quit joking.' We talked about it a little more, then hung up. Next thing I know he's at my place, asking if I was ready to go, and he drove us to the airport where he had his private jet waiting."

Ian interrupted her. "He had a private jet?" Like he could ever compete with that. Wait a minute, he wasn't competing with anyone over Sophie. They were just talking. That's it.

Yeah, right.

She nodded. "I told him, 'I don't have any luggage. You need to take me back home so I can pack.' But he said he would buy me whatever I needed and we got on the jet. We spent the whole weekend over there. Quite the adventure."

"Wow." Ian shook his head. He didn't know what to say. What kind of life had she really led? He'd heard a lot of rumors about her, most of them unflattering. It made him curious, made him want to get to know her better, figure her out. "That all sounds crazy."

"It was. Turns out *he* was crazy." Her expression grew somber and she averted her gaze. "Totally nuts. But that was a long time ago, when I lived in Miami." Those pretty eyes met his again, and he felt himself slowly start to drown in them.

"How long did you live there?" Damn it, he wanted to break the spell, needed to get out of whatever tangled web she seemed to weave around him with just her words. And her smile. Not to mention the sassy sparkle in her eyes. He wondered if this was what she did to all of the men she met.

71

And he realized that thought was pretty damn unfair. He had no idea how she conducted her private life. Rumors were just that—stories that could be true or could be all lies.

"Too long," she said quickly, as if she didn't want to talk about it, so he let the topic drop. She smiled at him again, resting her hands on her slim hips. "Want another drink, boss man?"

The last thing he needed was a drink and he definitely didn't want her to call him *boss man*. "No, I should get going. I have an early meeting tomorrow and I still need to go home and work out."

"What do you do to work out?"

Was her tone suggestive? Or was he just imagining things? "I usually run a couple of miles at least five nights a week."

"Cool. I like to run too." She grabbed his glass and dumped it into the sink behind the counter. "I overheard you talking earlier. Sorry about your breakup."

Okay, he didn't want to talk about *that*. With *her*. "No big deal."

"Weren't you two going to get married?"

"I never actually asked her but it was assumed." Part of his problem, he should've asked her. Should've given her a ring. Lord knew she hinted about it enough. But it never felt like the right time, and now he wondered if his doubts had something to do with realizing that maybe she wasn't the right woman. He'd certainly never know.

"That's tough, breaking up after being with someone for so long."

"Yeah, well, it happens." Ian shrugged, trying to act nonchalant, but it still stung. And not necessarily that he lost the girl, but *how* he lost the girl. How Nadia made him feel like an inadequate failure, when he'd never done anything else in his life but strive for perfection. Just when his life was coming together, Nadia had to kick him in the proverbial nuts and dump his ass. It sucked.

Chapter Two

Maybe Sophie shouldn't have mentioned his breakup. The minute she apologized his body language changed. His entire body tensed, his sensuous mouth drew tight. The playful light in his dark blue eyes dimmed. Like she had hit an invisible off switch, his entire mood went from cheerful to serious.

Too bad, considering she much preferred cheerful. And drunk and cute. She walked along the bar, collecting discarded glasses and dumping them into the sink. She'd never had a conversation with Ian before. Had only admired him from afar, knowing that nothing would ever come of it since he was her boss. And because he had a girlfriend he was practically married to. Now that the girlfriend was out of the picture and Sophie had him front and center at her bar, drunk and depressed, well, if she'd been the old Sophie, she'd probably figure out a way to take advantage of him. And then promptly do so.

But she wasn't that girl anymore. She wasn't going to sell herself out for another quick lay, only to be left wide open with a bleeding heart while whoever she'd just been with walked away from her and never looked back. No, she was on a different path now. She had plans to do something with her life and make something of herself. Once she finished working on herself, then she could attempt to find a man, establish a relationship that was real. True. To find someone who cared for her and wanted to do right by her, maybe even forever.

"You know, Sophie, I think I will take you up on your offer."

What, truly care for me and do right by me forever? Oh, yeah, that was her imaginary offer. Something *this* man wouldn't be interested in at all. For the life of her, she couldn't recall what he was talking about. "What do you mean?"

"Another drink. Same thing I had before, please." He smiled, dimples winking at her, and she wanted to melt into the floor. "I don't think I'm drunk enough."

"You wanna get drunk?" She cocked an eyebrow at him, grabbing a clean glass and filling it with ice. "How many drinks have you had?"

"This will be my fourth."

"Oh, I bet you still have a long way to go." She added a couple extra splashes of whiskey into the glass then poured cola into it before pushing it in front of him. "It's on the house, sir. Your money is no good here."

He chuckled, the sound of it sending a shiver down Sophie's spine, and took a long drink until the glass was less than half full when he set it on the counter. "You know, I never drink."

"Really?" She already knew this of course, since everyone loved to share any little tidbit about Ian Grey. She had a feeling most of his personal quirks were common knowledge amongst his employees.

Ian nodded. "Yep, I never drink. Ever. I don't like feeling out of control."

"So why are you drinking tonight?" She stood in front of him and his gaze met hers, his eyes burning with an intensity she'd never seen before. Something passed between them at that very moment, something dark and mysterious and sexual. Goose bumps broke out on her skin and she rubbed her arms, trying to ease the shivers that had come over her.

"Because my life already feels out of control so why not add to it?" He lifted the glass with his thumb and index finger and drained the rest of it in one swallow. "You know what's so funny? I could give a shit about not having Nadia in my life anymore."

Sophie wondered if that was really true, but she thought it wise to keep her opinions to herself.

"It's the fact that she screwed up my plans. I had plans, you know? My life was supposed to follow a particular order and now she kinked that all up by breaking it off with me." He shook his head, swirling the ice around in the glass.

"My life never goes according to plan," Sophie said, trying to make him feel better. Who had their entire life planned out? She'd been flying by the seat of her pants since she left home at seventeen. Sometimes she liked it that way, it made life more exciting. Most of the time though, it only seemed to cause her trouble.

"My life has always followed a plan. Now I don't know what to do." He looked completely and totally miserable. And also completely and totally like a lost and lonely little boy. For whatever silly reason, it touched her heart.

"Sometimes change is good. It makes you reevaluate your life and see what your priorities really are." At least that's what change did for her.

"I already know what my priorities are."

He was blowing her away with every statement he made. Was it natural to have your life so ordered, so mapped out? God, she didn't think so. The man definitely needed a change, he just didn't know it yet.

"Have you ever thought that maybe it just wasn't meant to be? That you can't always be in control of your life? That maybe all of this is a good thing? You are, after all, the man who has no time to be spontaneous. Maybe it'll do you some good to shake it up a little bit. Do something different for once in your life."

Ian looked away from her and stared at the countertop for a moment before he spoke. "Maybe you're right. Maybe a little change will do me some good."

"It doesn't hurt, you know." Their gazes met and held and her heart beat painfully. He was listening, really listening to her. And she liked it. "Letting go of the control you seem to hold so tightly over your life. You're so busy *planning* your life you're probably missing out on *living* it."

"You think so?" His voice was low, skimming over her nerve endings like velvet against bare skin, his eyes hot and suddenly sparkling with interest. For her? She wasn't quite sure.

"From everything you've told me tonight, yes, I do."

"So you've got me all figured out?" His dark eyebrows raised in challenge, the expression on his handsome face sexy as hell.

"Oh, far from it. Just trying to get you to relax, is all." He made her uncomfortable, in that edgy, aroused way she got when she was turned on. Their conversation was moving, shifting, straight towards unchartered territory. Territory she should step far away from if she knew what was good for her.

"Hey, Sophie?"

She whirled around and found Chuck standing next to her. She'd been so wrapped up in Ian that she hadn't even heard him approach. "Yeah, Chuck?"

"I hate to ask this of you but could you go back into the stockroom and clean out all the empty boxes? A delivery's coming in tomorrow and Randy unloaded a bunch of stuff back there. Forgot to clean it out when he left." Chuck shook his head. "Do you mind? It's not heavy work."

Disappointment filled her. She didn't want to leave Ian, afraid that if she left the bar he'd leave too. But she couldn't tell Chuck no. He was, after all, her manager. "No, I don't mind."

"Aw, Chuck, you're ruining our conversation."

Chuck laughed. "Sorry, Ian. Some of us around here have to *work* for a living."

"Ouch." Ian swirled the ice in his glass, his eyes meeting hers. His lips parted and she could feel his warm gaze travel over her lazily. "Nice talking to you, Sophie. Thanks for the advice."

"You're welcome, sir." She felt stupid sounding so formal but she didn't know what to say, how to act. Especially in front of Chuck.

Something flickered in his eyes and she wondered if he was disappointed by her formal tone. It was better, she told herself. She shouldn't be flirting with him, giving him advice. She couldn't help him when she could barely help herself. She didn't need his attention, anyway.

Though she wanted it.

₧)(₨

Sophie broke the empty boxes down one by one, throwing them into a growing pile. Her mind wandered, going over her conversation with Ian. Wishing circumstances were different, so she wouldn't feel so guilty harboring wicked feelings for her boss. A man who had total control over her own destiny, a situation she didn't want to put herself in.

That didn't stop her from being attracted to him, though. To recall the glint in his eyes when he looked at her, the sexy curve of his mouth. All that restrained power and muscle so nicely defined in his expensive suits.

She sighed, throwing the last box in the pile, and then wiped the sweat away from her forehead. He was a man who looked like he knew how to treat a woman right. A man who knew just how to touch her, knew just what to say to make her melt.

A man she had no business thinking about in such a manner. No matter how sexy he was, no matter how charming, he was off-limits.

There was a sudden shift in the air and Sophie knew the minute he walked into the storage room, smelled his unique masculine scent, heard the quiet click of the door closing. She stood a little straighter but didn't turn around. Wondered what he wanted exactly, though she already had an idea.

Telling herself he was off-limits seemed to have no meaning now that he was in the room with her, so close to her. If he made the first move, she knew she wouldn't stop him. Didn't want to stop him.

She didn't move, listened as he walked closer to her, could actually feel his body heat as he stood behind her, and she held her breath, ready for whatever he was going to do. It had been so long since she'd had sex, been with another man, and longing curled inside her, causing her entire body to tense with anticipation.

Big hands were suddenly at her waist and she expelled her held breath on a soft sigh, leaning her body against his. He was so solid and warm, his chest broad, his hands large and sure as they curled around her. Long fingers grazed her stomach, his face pressed into her neck and she closed her eyes, savoring the sensations of the man wrapped all around her.

"You smell delicious," he whispered in her ear, his lips so close they touched the tender skin. "I bet you taste even better."

Her heart fluttered wildly, a surge of moisture spreading between her thighs at his words. He pressed tiny kisses to her neck, his tongue darting out to lick, and she tilted her head to give him better access. She opened her eyes and watched as his hands moved up her stomach to cup her breasts, fingers gliding over her sensitive flesh, her nipples tightening with pleasure from his touch.

His hands smoothed downward, fingers tracing little circles over her stomach and she shivered, despite the close warmth of the storage room.

"You like that?" His teeth nibbled at her lobe and she bit her lip to keep the moan building inside of her from escaping.

She nodded in response and his free hand skittered up her arm. "I could tell. I'm giving you goose bumps."

Oh yes he was, and in more ways than one. Sophie tried to pull away from him, but he held her close, both arms settled on her waist, legs tucked around hers. "We shouldn't be doing this." She sounded weak, but who wouldn't sound weak when the sexiest, most handsome man she'd ever laid eyes on had his hands all over her, his mouth on her, driving her wild?

"You're the one who said I needed to be more spontaneous. More open to change." He brushed the hair away from her neck with gentle fingers, pressed his mouth against the back of it and she shivered again, wondering if anyone had ever kissed her there before. She had no idea the back of her neck was such an erogenous zone.

"I—I didn't think I was going to be a part of your spontaneous plan." She rested her arm over his, trying to stop him from sliding his hand beneath her shirt, but he did so anyway, his fingers now skimming bare flesh.

Ian chuckled, the sound reverberating through her. "From what you told me, spontaneous and plan don't go together."

He was right. Damn it. "Just this once, then," she said, giving in so easily, a little disgusted with herself for doing so. She closed her eyes as both of his hands cupped her breasts, thumbs rubbing against her lace-covered nipples. "It'll be our spontaneous secret."

"Right," he panted, his breath hot in her ear. "Just this once."

Sophie turned her head to the side and his mouth found hers, surprising her. The kiss was gentle, his lips soft and smooth as they moved against hers, his tongue sliding into her mouth with ease. She turned in his arms to face him, pressing her body against his as she threw herself into the kiss. She didn't hold back, reveling in the delicious sensation of his mouth connecting with her mouth, his tongue dancing with her tongue.

She realized he'd somehow gotten rid of his suit jacket and tie. His erection brushed against her stomach, setting her body on fire while his hands snuck around to her back, looking for the clasp of her bra. She broke the kiss to gaze up at him.

"We can't do this in here."

"Why not?" He was so focused on trying to disentangle her from her bra, which he still hadn't figured out clasped in the front, he didn't even bother to look up at her. She stood her ground, though, arms stiff at her sides so he couldn't undress her. His gaze finally met hers, smoldering and frustrated. "If we're going to be spontaneous, we may as well go for it."

Sophie looked around, her gaze lingering on the door. Anyone could walk into the room at any time, though she doubted it would happen. For one thing, it was late, only Chuck and LuAnn the cocktail waitress worked the bar, and it was fully stocked. The only reason anyone would need to come back there would be to get more alcohol. The likelihood of that was slim.

But still...

"I'll lock the door." Ian must have been watching her watch the door she realized when he released her. He strode towards it, turned the lock into place and then faced her. Hands rested on his lean hips, contemplating her with an unreadable expression on his face.

She knew then there was no going back. And she didn't want to, either.

Chapter Three

Sophie stood frozen, her breath coming in short pants, her body still reacting from his kiss and touch. *I could back out right now and get out of here. Pretend like it never happened. It would be better that way. Easier.*

"Do you want to leave?" He must have read her mind.

Yes. "No," she answered. Why did she say that?

Ian started walking towards her, his stride sure, his expression...*hmm*. It was the expression of a man intent on having his way with a woman. His lids heavy, eyes slumberous, his mouth full, almost vulnerable looking and damp from their shared kiss. He looked ready to devour her in one gulp. Her entire body trembled with anticipation, her nipples painfully hard beneath her bra, panties drenched. *It's because it's been so long. I can't remember the last time I had sex. My body craves it*—anyone *would do.*

Yeah right. More like she'd been craving *him* from the first moment she saw him. And now all her dirty little dreams would come true. For a price, such as her dignity.

"Come on," Ian said, taking her hand.

He led her through the deep recesses of the storage room, past the many rows of shelves that stocked all of the liquor bottles, paper products and extras, until they reached the deepest, darkest corner of the room. Ian pressed her against the wall, his hard body rubbing against her, his gaze locking with hers.

"You're drunk," Sophie said. She wanted him to realize she knew exactly where this was going—absolutely nowhere. And wanted to remind herself that maybe this wasn't such a good idea after all. Not that she was going to stop it from happening.

Yet again proof that she was too weak when it came to handsome, charming men.

He smiled a slow sexy grin that thrilled her right down to her toes. "I know." He touched her nose with the tip of his index finger, trailed it down her cheek to trace her lips. "Does that bother you?"

"Makes me wonder what your real motive is for being here." She glanced about the dark corner, felt his fingers move down to curve around her neck. His touch felt so good. Too good. "Why you're in a dark corner with me when you've hardly spoken to me since I started working here."

"I run this entire hotel. I hardly have time to speak to the employees who report directly to me, let alone every single one." He brought her closer to him. "Not that I haven't noticed you."

"You have?" Hope rose within her then fell just as quickly in disappointment. Of course he'd noticed her. The minute she walked into the hotel looking for a job her reputation followed right behind her. She couldn't shake that thing if she tried, and Lord knew she tried. It didn't help that one of the cocktail waitresses knew her from the Wily Fox, so she spread the rumors of her past extravagant lifestyle, all of her many boyfriends. So embarrassing.

Yet here she was living up to her reputation yet again. Allowing herself to be seduced—by the boss, no less—in the storage room of the bar where she worked. Like the gullible girl she'd always been.

When would she ever learn?

Ian nodded. "I couldn't help but notice you. You're beautiful." His lips brushed against hers, slowly, deliberately chaste, powerfully seductive. She melted against him, her arms wrapping around his waist, holding on to him for fear she'd fall to the ground if she didn't.

His hands were at the front of her shirt, undoing the buttons, pushing her shirt open to reveal white-lace-encased breasts. He broke the kiss, his gaze drinking her in, his fingers swirling around her already hard nipples. "It's been so long..."

Her head snapped up, eyes meeting his. "What do you mean?" Been so long since what? He'd been with his girlfriend for the last five years. Surely, he wasn't referring to sex.

Ian shook his head, a grim smile on his face. "Nothing. Let's get you out of this." With a nimble flick of his fingers the front snap of her bra came undone, her breasts falling into his hands. He smoothed his thumbs over her nipples and she threw her head back against the wall, closing her eyes. Every time he touched her, looked at her, it was as if electric sparks went shooting across her nerve endings. She didn't remember ever reacting to a man like this, her entire being yearning for him. Sophie had always been the type to treat sex lightly, used it for fun, and of course, to get off.

Tonight she wanted to have sex with Ian Grey to share a piece of her with him and to claim a part of him for her alone. It dawned on her she didn't care if he was using her to get over his girlfriend, didn't really care if they never saw each other again.

Okay, that last part was a lie. But she wasn't going to think about that right now. Couldn't...

And who wanted to, when the very man she wanted a piece of just bent over her to draw her nipple into his mouth, sucking gently, his hand caressing her other breast. She moaned, sank her fingers into his soft dark hair and held him to her, never wanting him to stop. His other hand moved down her body to the edge of her short skirt, lifting it up to slide beneath, cupping her lace-covered bottom.

Ian lifted his head and gazed into her eyes as his hand slipped to her front, pressing against her sex. She gasped, wanting to close her eyes but couldn't, trapped by the intensity of his stare. The intent of his fingers as they tucked beneath her panties, dipping into her soaking wet pussy. His blue eyes flared as he touched her, testing her wetness, and she spread her legs, giving him better access.

"You're wet." He said it as if he couldn't believe it. Was he crazy? All he had to do was look at her and her panties were drenched.

"For you," she said, unable to stop herself. Why not let him know how much he turned her on? When was the last time his now ex-girlfriend told him that? From the way he was talking and acting, Sophie had a feeling it had been a long time.

He leaned in and kissed her hard, pressing her against the wall even harder. His finger went to work inside her folds, searching, finding her clit, touching it lightly. She moaned against his mouth, her hands moving to the front of his shirt to unbutton it.

It parted with each undone button and her fingers connected with warm male flesh. She tested it, smoothing her hands over his hair-roughened skin. His chest was broad, muscles firm. She stripped him of his shirt, running her hands over his muscular arms, up to his broad shoulders. He felt good, so big and strong. His clean and spicy scent filled her nostrils. The lingering flavor of whiskey on his tongue as it stroked hers teased her taste buds. And what his fingers were doing down south, oh my. She had a feeling she was going to come any minute.

"Touch me," he said against her lips, his voice harsh, ragged, thrusting his hips against hers. As if she had as much affect on him as he did on her.

Sophie stroked his erect cock through his trousers with firm fingers. His heat seared her and her fingers curled around him, tearing a groan from deep inside his chest.

He dropped in front of her, on his knees, his hands pushing her skirt up so it bunched around her waist. He stared at her for a moment, his breathing fast and loud. His hands rested at her hips, fingers pulling on the waistband of her lace panties, and he tugged them down, revealing her to him.

"Oh God," he whispered, eyeing her naked pussy eagerly. His gaze lifted, meeting hers. "You're completely bare."

She nodded, sinking her fingers into his thick dark hair.

His warm hands curved over her hips, ran down her thighs and then moved up inside them, spreading her legs wider. He breathed against her, so hot, making her tingle, and she closed her eyes, leaning heavily against the wall.

"I can see everything." He moaned, ran a single finger over her slit, and she moaned as well.

"Like what you see?" she couldn't help but ask. Didn't that dopey girlfriend of his ever do anything as simple as wax down there? The man acted like he'd never seen a pussy before in his life.

"Oh yeah." He leaned in close, breathing deeply, and closed his eyes. "Do you want me to go down on you?"

He actually had to ask? If he didn't thrust his tongue or fingers inside her quickly, she was going to *die*. "Yes. *Please.*"

His thumbs spread her swollen pussy lips, opening her wide to his gaze. She wasn't embarrassed to have herself examined so closely, didn't even care, so eager to have him lick her, drive his tongue inside her. Never before had she wanted a man so much, so fast.

And then his tongue was there, tentative against her throbbing center, licking her slowly. She closed her eyes, allowing the sensations to take over, carry her away. He licked and stroked, his tongue like velvet against her hot sensitive skin, and she clutched tighter at his head.

His hands came around to squeeze her bottom, his lips closing around her clit, and he sucked it into his mouth. She bucked against him, nearly fainting with pleasure when his teeth lightly nibbled on the sensitive nub. Long fingers stroked down the crack of her ass, stopping at her pussy, and then they thrust deep inside her, making her cry out.

"Did that hurt?" His mouth tickled her pussy when he spoke.

She shook her head, knees weak as his fingers thrust in and out of her slowly. "It feels good."

"I want to make you come." He sucked on her clit again as his fingers still pumped inside her.

"Keep doing what you're doing and it's guaranteed."

He smiled against her, then his mouth opened, sucking on her. His fingers moved faster and she clutched at his head, cramming his face into her.

"Oh, yes, yes," she murmured, not even trying to keep herself quiet. Not able to care if anyone found them at this moment. All she could focus on was Ian's mouth on her, his fingers inside her, his lips sucking on her clit so hard he was going to make her come...

And she did, crying out when it hit her, her fingers tight in his hair. His fingers stayed deep inside her and his tongue continued to play with her clit. All of it so much, so fast, so intense, she couldn't take it anymore.

Sophie tugged on his hair, pulling his face away from her, and he looked up at her, his chin glistening with her juices. He removed his fingers from her and dragged them back up the crack of her ass, tickling at her anus. She jumped at the delicious sensation it brought forth.

"Jesus, you're like my every fantasy come to life." His dark gaze drank her in, his eyes appreciative as he stood to his full height. His hands kneaded her buttocks, the tent in the front of his pants an indication that he needed some satisfaction and fast. And she was just the one to give it to him.

Ian held her close, his own wildly beating heart drowning out the sound of her harsh breathing. Her body still trembled in his arms and he marveled at her response. Nadia had certainly never reacted like *that*. He'd felt Sophie's orgasm deep inside, her inner walls milking his fingers, the gush of wetness that surged at his lips when she came. He'd almost shot off himself at the sensation of it all.

She rubbed against him, her pebbled nipples making contact with his chest, and his cock surged, reminding him that he had unfinished business to tend to. That is, if Sophie was still willing...

Her slim fingers trailing back down to press over his crotch indicated she was still willing. Those nimble fingers undoing the button of his pants and tugging down his zipper more than indicated she was willing. And oh shit when her fingers curled around his hard flesh, he jerked in her hand.

"I want you to take me," she murmured into his chest, then licked him long and slow. Like a satisfied cat. He shivered again.

"Take you?"

Sophie's head lifted, her blue eyes meeting his, silent. Her hand still curled around his cock, stroking up and down, making him pulse with need. Her lips parted and she stood on tiptoe, bringing her mouth close to his ear.

"I want you to fuck me, Ian."

He didn't even hesitate, reaching for his wallet from his back pocket with a jerk and opening it. One token packet was tucked inside the leather and he pulled it out. She helped him, pushed first his pants then his underwear down his hips. His clothing landed at his ankles and he realized it didn't faze him, what they were about to do. In a storage room at his hotel. He wasn't even worried about being caught in the throes of sexual passion with Sophie Kincaid. He was too focused on her and what they were about to do.

He heard her sharp intake of breath and caught her staring at him, watching his impossibly hard cock twitch with impatience.

"Wow." Her lips parted and he could imagine thrusting his cock in between them, the warm cavern of her mouth milking him. Nadia had *never* given him a blow job, proclaiming them as "disgusting" and "vulgar".

He had a feeling Sophie would suck his dick and like it. A lot.

"Come here," he said with a growl, rolling the condom on.

She did so and he grabbed her by the waist, hauling her to him, her legs wrapping around his middle. Her warm wet pussy pressed so close to his sheathed cock and with one thrust, he was inside.

Sophie cried out and he grasped her buttocks, propping her up against the wall. He moved within her, her inner walls tightening around him, gripping his cock like a velvet fist. God, he was going to lose it. He was this close to spurting off in her tight wet heat already.

"You feel so good."

Ian opened his eyes at her words to find her watching him, her lower lip caught in her teeth, her eyes glazed. Her cheeks were flushed and blonde wisps of hair clung to her face. She was beautiful, so beautiful and he couldn't resist. His lips met hers in a searing kiss, their tongues eager, teeth clashing. He pressed her even harder against the wall, regretfully tearing his mouth away from hers.

"Don't move," he murmured.

She listened to him, plastering herself against the wall, and he slowly pushed himself deep within her, staying there for a moment before pulling out. Then he thrust inside her again. Her head tilted back, eyes closing as a low moan of ecstasy escaped her.

"Oh, yes," she said, her hands flat along the wall, legs locked tight around him. He increased his pace, the friction between them sending off enough sparks he was surprised they didn't burst into flames. His balls drew up tight to his body, his dick surged and he knew he was gonna come. Gonna explode inside of her like he never had before.

With a groan he climaxed, his semen gushing from him like a geyser, filling the annoying condom as he thrust again and again and again. She slumped against him, her inner walls contracting around him as a low moan tore from her throat.

"Oh, my God," she whispered, her lips brushing his throat after it was all said and done, the both of them satisfied.

He lifted his head, smiled down at her, fingers lingering on her warm cheek. "You can say that again."

"Oh, my God." Sophie smiled and he withdrew from her, pulling the used condom off him. He clutched it in his hand, not sure of what to do with it. "I'll take that."

He handed her the condom carefully, and she walked over to a small garbage can and threw it inside. He watched her, noticed how sexy she looked in her high-heeled sandals, her skirt up around her waist, her pretty ass pink from being pressed against the wall.

As if she knew he was staring right at her ass, she yanked her skirt down, smoothing the fabric with her palms. He could see it on her face, could see it in her eyes. She was feeling regret, he could tell. Probably wasn't sure how to react. Hell, he wasn't sure how he should react either.

"That was very...spontaneous," she finally said, tugging on the hem of her skirt.

Ian pulled his underwear and pants up. "I'll say."

"We probably shouldn't have done that." Her gaze met his, reluctant.

"Why not?"

Sophie shrugged. "That entire boss, employee thing. The fact that I'm a bartender, and I know I'm not really deserving of your attention."

"What the hell are you talking about?"

She smiled, a winsome smile. A little lonely, a little sad, that smile said it all. "You know exactly what I'm talking about. You know what you get when you get with me. Easy sex, no strings. I'm sure you've heard the rumors about my past."

"You're saying they're true?" He buttoned up his shirt, surprised by her admissions, wondering why she was bringing all of this up now.

"I'm not denying them." She clasped her bra and buttoned her shirt too. "I've done things in my past I'm not proud of. This probably wasn't too smart of a move either. I'm sorry, Ian."

"There's nothing to apologize for. Maybe we should get together again, go to dinner..."

She stopped him from talking any further, pressing her index finger against his mouth, and he shut up. "No, let's not ruin it. Let's leave it at this. A lovely memory and no more."

Ian watched her go, perplexed. Wondering why she thought so low of herself. Wishing he knew her better, wishing he could figure her out. Knowing it wasn't smart to think any of this. But he couldn't help it.

He still wanted her. Even after everything they'd done, even though she'd walked out of the room, he wanted her. More than he wanted her before they had sex. He thought fucking her would get her out of his system, but he'd been wrong.

Now she was so deep inside him he didn't think he'd ever get her out.

Chapter Four

Ian had no business doing what he was about to do.

No, he shouldn't be doing it at all. He should turn his car around and head back home, to another lonely night. By himself, no one to keep him company except his television or his laptop.

Shit, that was way too freaking depressing. No way did he want to go back to his empty house and face *that*. Face the loneliness in his life, the monotony of it all. After the breakup with Nadia, he'd realized just how boring he'd become. Hell, he didn't half blame her for leaving. He probably would've left himself.

And then the night with Sophie two weeks ago, that unbelievable moment in the storage room that had turned his life completely upside down. He'd never had a woman so responsive, so sensual, so explosive in his arms before. He told himself he didn't want a relationship, didn't want anything special with Sophie Kincaid.

He just wanted to experience her again. To hold her in his arms, kiss her, taste her, fuck her...

Ian never thought in terms of *fucking* a woman. He was too damn polite, and after so many years with Nadia, being in a "proper" relationship, he definitely didn't think about *fucking* a woman. He was supposed to make love, have sex, whatever.

Funny how all he could think about was fucking Sophie's brains out since he'd had her. How much she'd probably like it if he said that in her ear. *I want to fuck you.*

So that's why he drove towards her apartment at ten o'clock at night. He'd looked up her address earlier at work, accessed the Human Resources files. No one ever questioned him when he did so, for he did it all the time. When he'd done so earlier, though, it felt sordid. Wrong and more than a little sleazy. But he did it anyway, because he wanted to know where she lived. So he could go see her later.

Hell, he was a dirty bastard.

She didn't live in the best part of Oakland, but he wasn't surprised. He'd heard the stories about her starting over, running away from whatever trouble she'd gotten into in Miami. Then there had been the trouble she'd had before she started at the hotel, when she'd worked at a strip club. Rumor had it she'd been a stripper a time or two to earn extra cash. He had no idea if that was true. Financial trouble and a crappy boyfriend had also been the rumor as to why she lost her job. From the looks of where she lived, he didn't doubt the financial part.

Ian pulled up in front of the apartment building and stared up at it in mock horror. Shit, it was worse than he thought. She lived in a total dump. The place looked dirty, the parking lot full of old cars, a bunch of tough-looking young men standing around, watching him as he got out of his car. He was almost afraid to leave his Lexus so close to a bunch of thugs, even though he could lock it and put the security alarm on, no problem.

Like that would stop them if they wanted to steal it.

Deciding that even a stolen car wouldn't stop him from seeing Sophie Kincaid again, Ian hit the keyless remote and stalked towards her building, relieved to see that at least she lived upstairs. Safer, he assumed. The stairwell rattled as he walked up the steps and he pulled at his too-tight collar. The heat wave that had swept the Bay Area left the night air a sweltering eighty-five degrees. Not even the breezes off the San Francisco Bay helped ease the temperatures.

He hoped Sophie had a decent air conditioner. From the looks of the place, he doubted it.

Sophie glanced up from the sink at the sound of the doorbell. She turned off the water and patted her face dry, cocking her ear towards the front of the apartment. Did her doorbell really ring?

She strode into her bedroom, glancing at the clock on the nightstand. Who would be ringing her doorbell at ten o'clock on a Thursday night? Maybe it hadn't been her doorbell. The walls were thin in these old apartments, and occasionally she would hear knocks on the door of her neighbor's. Maybe it was someone coming to visit them.

She also heard lots of screaming sex coming from her neighbors below her. In fact, one bout had been particularly loud a few nights ago and she'd ended up masturbating to their shouts. Her mind filled with images of Ian Grey pumping his thick cock inside of her. Being fucked by his marvelous fingers, eaten by his generous mouth.

Just thinking about it right now made her wet.

A soft knock sounded on her door and she stiffened, nervous. There was nobody who would visit her at this time of night. Her only friends were a small group of fellow employees, and she was too embarrassed to invite them over. Her mother never left the house after sundown. Who could it be?

Sophie crept to the front door and peeked into the peephole, curious to know who stood on her doorstep. She immediately slumped against the door in disbelief at seeing who was on the other side.

Ian Grey? The man of her fantasies? The man who made her mouth water and her panties damp at the mere thought of him?

She looked through the peephole again, watching as he tugged at the collar of his crisp shirt, loosening the knot of his tie. He must've come straight over from work, still wearing a suit in the stifling heat. He looked good enough to eat.

Even though she was clad in only a revealing silky pink nightgown, she opened the door cautiously, her heart beating hard. "What are you doing here?"

"Is that any way to greet your boss?" His expression appeared about as jumpy as she felt, though she did notice the appreciative gleam in his eyes as he drank her in.

Hah. "What is my boss doing on my doorstep in the middle of the night?"

He ignored her question and gestured at the door. "May I come in?"

"Sure." She watched as he walked into her place, and she shut the door slowly, trying to gather her thoughts. She filled with shame at the shabbiness of the old apartment, at her lack of furniture or knickknacks. The place more than anything was just a spot to crash, a place to get ready before she left for work. She tried to avoid hanging out there as much as possible. She *never* invited anyone over.

"Nice apartment," Ian said as he looked around.

Sophie wanted to laugh out loud. What a liar. The place was a shit hole. "Yeah, right."

He walked over to the giant box turned upside down that acted as a temporary table. "Interesting furniture choice."

She shrugged, willing herself not to flush with embarrassment. "I just moved in, I haven't had a chance to furniture shop yet." That and the fact she had absolutely no money for furniture.

"The place has a lot of potential."

Enough with the small talk. "Why are you here, Ian?"

His expression grew serious. "I needed to see you."

"You needed to see me? For what? And why now? Couldn't this have waited until tomorrow?"

Ian shook his head, taking a couple of steps towards her, and she grew weak as he drew closer. "No."

"Then what's so urgent that you needed to see me now?" She was no fool—she knew why he was there. She just wanted to hear him say it.

"This," he said, stopping just before her, his arms sliding around her waist to pull her to him. His erection throbbed against her lower body, his eyes blazed into hers and she closed her eyes, reveling in the sensation of his body pressed next to hers again.

Sophie forced her eyes open and cleared her throat. "I thought we were only going to do this once. Remember?"

Ian buried his face in her hair. "I guess I'm not very good at keeping my promises."

His hands smoothed up and down her back, fingers lingering on her bare skin, and she shivered in his arms.

"Ian, you should go." Her voice sounded weak and she didn't really mean it. Being in his arms again, feeling his solid muscular warmth pressed up against her, was too delicious to turn away.

"You're all I think about," he murmured, his lips at her temple, kissing her there. The gesture was so tender she closed her eyes against the emotions that surged at his touch. "You're distracting me from my work and that *never* happens."

Sophie smiled faintly, resting her hands on his chest. "I don't mean to distract you."

His hands cupped her bottom. "Show me your bedroom, Sophie. I want to see your five-hundred-dollar sheets."

Pleasure bloomed in her chest, thrilled that he remembered. Silly as it was, it did make her feel good. She disentangled herself from his arms. "Ian..."

He smiled, looking beyond her at the short hall that led to her bedroom, before meeting her gaze once more. "I like to hear you say my name, even when you're irritated with me. Say it again."

She rolled her eyes. "Please. Now you're just being ridiculous."

"No, I'm a man with a supreme hard-on and the only person who can help relieve it is you." He started towards the hallway. "Come on, sweetheart, let's go check out your sheets."

"Ian! Do you think you can just walk in here and tell me what to do? Just because you're my boss at work doesn't mean you're my boss at home."

He stopped in his tracks and crossed his arms in front of his impressive chest. "You're telling me if I touched you right now I wouldn't find you wet and ready for me?"

She was dripping just at his words but she couldn't admit that. Certainly didn't *want* to admit it.

"Sophie," he said, a tantalizing light in his eyes as he took one step closer to her. "Come here."

Her anger evaporating, she walked towards him, her feet light as air. Thrilling pleasure rose up inside her at the animalistic expression on his face, the commanding tone of his deep voice.

"That's more like it," he said, his arms drawing her closer, his erection settling against her belly. She couldn't stop herself from touching him there, fingers lingering on his hard shaft. Desperate to undress him, see him naked, have her way with him.

"If you really want me to go, I'll leave," he whispered in her ear, his tongue licking at the sensitive spot behind it. "I'm not going to force myself on you if you don't want me."

If you don't want me. The craziest words she'd ever heard. "Ian…"

"God, Sophie, I've been going crazy thinking about you. Imagining touching you again, fucking you on your expensive sheets." He nuzzled her temple with his face, the gesture tender, endearing. "No distractions, no worries about anyone walking in, interrupting us. Just the two of us together, all night long."

Thank goodness he held her or else she'd be a puddle on the floor. Her entire body throbbed at his words, her breasts tight with wanting, her pussy wet and ready for him.

His hands stroked up and down her back, nudging her so close to him it was as if they were fused together. "I've been thinking about you too," she admitted.

He breathed deep, his chest swelling beneath her cheek, and she turned her head, pressing her mouth against the fabric of his shirt. She wanted to gobble him up, consume him. If only for one more night, then so be it.

"Let's go," Ian said, taking her hand.

She followed him back to her tiny bedroom, ashamed yet again at the lack of furnishings in her place. She only had the bed, not even a dresser or bedside tables. She stashed all of her clothes in the blessedly large walk-in closet her bedroom had, and the door was shut against the exploding disaster of it all.

"Purple?" He cocked an eyebrow at her, referring to her color choice for the sheets.

Sophie bent at the knee and ran her hand over the smooth cool sheets. "Not too feminine, not too masculine."

"Just right," he ended with a smile. He glanced about the small room, his eyes settling on the large fan sitting on the floor. "Does that thing work?"

"Yes. Turn it on, if you want to."

He did so, and she admired the flex of his legs and buttocks when he bent down. He was gorgeous, rich, sexy and amazing sexually. What the hell did he really see in her?

"No air conditioning in this place?"

"It's old, doesn't work very well. And normally we don't need it that much here with the mild summers."

"Nothing mild about this summer. Or at least the last few days." Ian shrugged out of his jacket and undid his tie, throwing it on the floor. He began unbuttoning his shirt, each undone button revealing his muscular chest, and Sophie's mouth watered at the sight of him. Watching him undress so casually while she stood there drooling over him like a giant treat she couldn't wait to dive into. Anticipation thrummed in her veins and, barely able to contain herself, she tore off her nightgown.

His fingers went to the fly of his trousers and she rushed towards him, swatting his hands away. Her fingers tucked beneath his waistband, grazing against the hot flesh of his belly, and she led him towards the bed, sitting down on it.

Ian still stood, gazing down at her, his eyes hot, his chest lifting and falling rapidly. She watched him as she undid the button and tugged the zipper down, the sound of it seeming to fill the quiet room. She pushed at his trousers and they fell in a heap to the floor, revealing his black boxer briefs. His cock strained against the thin fabric, the smell of his arousal tickling her nostrils, musky male and intoxicating. Licking her lips, she shoved his underwear off his hips, down his legs, and he stepped out of the pile of clothes at his ankles, also ridding himself of his socks.

Wonderfully naked, she thought as she let her gaze wander over him from head to toe. His penis, thick and long, growing from a patch of black curling pubic hair. A glistening drop of moisture wept from the tip of it and she dipped forward, licking it away.

He gasped then growled, his hips jerking towards her. "Jesus, Sophie."

"I've been dying to taste you," she admitted, her lips wrapping around the head of his cock.

Ian thrust his hands into her hair, holding her head steady as she swirled her tongue around him and pushed his cock inside her mouth as far as he could go. She released him, licked his length, tickled his balls with the tip of her tongue and he groaned.

"More?" she asked, playing innocent.

He nodded, guiding her head and mouth back to the plum-shaped head of his penis. "Definitely more."

She sucked and licked, nibbled and played with his cock, loving his taste, loving even more his reactions to her. His hands tightened in her hair and he thrust his hips rhythmically, fucking her mouth, really. She wanted to give him pleasure, she wanted to hear him scream with it, wanted him to be weak with it. All because of her and the power she held over him.

The same sexual power he held over *her*.

"I'm gonna come," he said, forcing her to look up at him.

She continued to pump him in and out of her mouth, smiling when she heard the low groan come from deep within him. His balls were tight against his groin, his entire body tense and she knew he was close. She wanted him to explode in her mouth, was desperate for it.

"I don't want to come like this, Sophie," he mumbled, his voice weak. "Please, I want to be inside you."

Ignoring him, she sucked hard, her hand gripping the base of him, pumping his shaft. He climaxed without warning, his semen spurting into her mouth. She drank from him and gentled her hold on his cock, licking at his length as the shudders that overtook his body slowly subsided.

"Damn..."

Sophie released him and he attacked her, pushing her back against the mattress, his big body covering hers. He was damp and sweaty and already semi-erect again, and she shivered with want.

"You are amazing," he said, kissing her, his mouth so wet, so hot on hers.

She opened her mouth to him, and his tongue darted in with ease, tangling with her own. The kiss was carnal, sizzling with electricity. Made her whimper for more, her legs restless as they shifted against his. Her body grew sticky with sweat just like his and she slicked her hands over his shoulders, down his damp arms. It was so hot in her bedroom, the fan not enough to cool their heated bodies. She pushed at him, forcing him to roll over so she was on top.

"Hmmm, perfect," he murmured, his hands cupping her breasts, thumbs playing with her erect nipples.

She arched her chest towards his mouth, feeling his cock brush against her wet folds, and she was overcome with the urge to impale herself on him.

"Do you have condoms?" he asked, his eyes blazing into hers.

She gazed down at him, her hair falling around her face as she shook her head no. "I'm on the pill, though."

He looked towards the pile of clothing on the floor. "I have a couple in my pocket."

"Ian." She placed her hand on his cheek, turning his head so he looked at her. "I'm safe, I have a feeling you're safe. I want to *feel* you when you're inside me. Please."

He groaned his answer, closed his eyes and thrust his hips towards her as she guided him inside. He stretched her, filled her so completely and she leaned forward, over him. His hand grabbed hers, fingers entwined and just like that, she felt connected to him. Something she'd never experienced before with a man during sex.

"Open your eyes, Sophie."

She did, amazed at all of the emotion she saw shining in his, the tender expression on his face. She bent towards him even more, her hair enclosing them, and he kissed her, his lips gentle and searching, his free hand coming up to cup her cheek.

Tears threatened to shed and she shook her head, stunned by it all. This didn't make any sense, none of it made any sense. How could she feel so strongly for a man she didn't really know? She couldn't blame it on the hot sex they shared.

She'd shared plenty of good sex with men in the past, though none of it had felt like *this*. Like it felt with Ian.

By the intensity in his gaze, the gentle way he touched her, she had a feeling he felt the same way too.

She sat back up and began to ride him, sliding herself up and down his rigid cock. Their hands still clasped together, his other hand played with first one breast, then the other. He pinched her nipples and she gasped at the pleasure/pain sensation. He finally released her hand and gripped her by the hips, guiding her on his cock, and they moved in tandem. Her climax threatened to erupt, take over her body. Make her lose control.

Ian stilled beneath her and she groaned, her body shivering with the onslaught of her orgasm, her inner walls clenching around him. She cried out his name and he thrust deep, spurting hot semen inside her, filling her.

Completing her.

Chapter Five

Yet again Ian was doing something he shouldn't.

Summoning a woman to his office for the sole purpose of seeing her again. Using his job, his position as a front so he could see Sophie, ask her what happened, explain to her how he felt.

After his surprise visit to her apartment two weeks ago had turned into an all-night sex fest, he'd asked her to stay with him at his house for the weekend. He had the time off, she had the time off, he thought it would be the perfect opportunity to spend more time with her, get to know each other.

The two solid days they had shared together had been amazing. He'd never felt closer to a woman, not even Nadia, whom he'd been with for so long. He and Sophie had never left the house and spent the majority of their time together naked, laughing, talking, eating, making love. He'd never been more sore and exhausted in his life.

Never been happier either.

His parents had shown up unexpectedly on Sunday afternoon and she fled without saying a word to him. One minute she'd been there, the next minute she was gone. He'd left her alone for a few days, didn't want to push, and then he'd gotten caught up with work. He even left for a week to a conference in Florida.

Next thing he knew two weeks had passed and he hadn't heard a peep from her.

Part of it was his own fault and he could take responsibility. Not like his fingers were broken, he knew how to make a phone call. His legs weren't broken either—he should've stopped by the bar to talk to her. But if he did that then he'd have to do something else to her. Like pull her into his arms and kiss her, run his hands all over her beautiful body before stripping her of her clothing. Stroke her into a frenzy then bury himself deep inside her. Make her cry out with pleasure right before she came.

Shit, he never once in his life felt like this over a woman before. She drove him nuts, made him crazy, made him horny, was always on his mind. He liked it too. Hell, he liked *her*. After spending so much time with her, two days of talking with her, making love to her, he realized just how much.

A forever kind of how much, that's what.

It didn't scare him, either. It had scared him with Nadia, had scared him with other women he'd been involved with in the past. Being close to his mid-thirties, he'd assumed he'd find the right woman soon. At one point, he'd thought Nadia had been the right woman but something always niggled at him in the back of his mind. A seed of doubt that grew and grew as time passed.

With Sophie, there was no doubt. She was the woman for him. She had to be.

Now Ian just needed to convince her.

෨ඥ

"The boss man wants to see you."

Sophie glanced up at Chuck and set another clean glass in the row of already clean glasses behind the counter. "What are you talking about?"

"Mister Ian Grey himself has summoned you to his office. Better go see what he wants before the five o'clock rush shows up."

Nerves clamored inside of her as she walked out of the bar, and she twisted her hands together. She hadn't seen Ian in over two weeks, not after they spent an amazing two days together at his house. She hadn't been able to turn him down the morning after his spontaneous visit to her apartment. She'd been sleepy and sated after a full night of lovemaking, and he'd looked so handsome, so appealing when he'd asked her to come over. Considering it was her one weekend a month she had off, she took him up on the offer.

It had been two days of luxurious living, decadent sex, delicious food and overall pleasant company. Surprisingly, she and Ian had a lot in common, similar tastes in movies, music, books and even politics. Yes, he was intense and focused, but he was also sweet and funny. And amazing in bed.

Beyond amazing. He did things to her, made her feel in ways she'd never done or felt before. The entire weekend had been like a dream, the best dream she'd ever had, until Sunday afternoon when his parents stopped by for a surprise visit.

Not even waiting around to meet the folks, Sophie got out of there fast, uncomfortable with the situation. She didn't want to feel like she didn't measure up, didn't want to see the disappointment flicker in their eyes when they met the woman their son was boning. Because that's all it was, there wasn't a relationship. It was just based on sex. Incredible, earth-shaking, mind-blowing sex.

Besides, she *didn't* measure up. She was a bartender with no direction in her life, too lazy to pursue anything that would better herself and her future. She certainly wasn't worthy of such a man's intentions, didn't know why Ian seemed so interested in her.

He didn't treat her like she was just a fuck, but maybe that was his way. Charming and sweet and tender, he had treated her like a princess all weekend long. Feeding her breakfast in bed, giving her bone-melting massages, washing her in his giant whirlpool bathtub before he made love to her. He acted like nothing was too good for her. It had been wonderful.

Like a fool she'd run out on him and never looked back. She didn't contact him, acted as if she wasn't even interested in him anymore. All of it lies. She was dying to call him, touch him, kiss him. Wanted to feel his hands on her again, stripping her naked, leaving her open and vulnerable to him. For once in her life, she *wanted* to be vulnerable to a man, let him see all of her. Not afraid of how he'd treat her.

Yet he'd ignored her too. She'd barely seen him the past two weeks, which hurt. Didn't he care enough to try and contact her? Of course, she cared but didn't contact *him*. So turnabout seemed like fair play. Damn it.

And now he'd called her to his office. Who knew what he wanted? She was so nervous she could barely walk. She only hoped he wouldn't fire her. She really needed to keep this job. Needed to have some sort of stability in her life, even if she couldn't have him.

Sophie realized then, as she walked to his office, she *did* want him. She wanted to see if they could make something work. He probably wasn't interested, but if she got up enough nerve, she might mention it to him. See what his reaction would be.

The lobby for the executive offices was huge, like a cavern, and she smiled at the secretary who sat behind the polished desk set in the exact middle of the room.

"Ian Grey asked me to see him?"

The secretary nodded and picked up the ringing phone. "You can go ahead and see him. His office is right there," she said, pointing her finger towards a door.

Sophie went to the door and opened it, peeking her head inside. Ian sat at his desk, his dark head dipped down, reading something. She stepped inside the doorway and shut it behind her with a silent click, content to watch him before he noticed her.

The suit jacket was long gone, his normally pressed and crisp, white, button-down shirt rumpled, the blue silk tie loosened. Sleeves unbuttoned and rolled up to reveal strong forearms, thick wrists, his beautiful hands. Hands that had been all over her body, inside her body, bringing her such intense pleasure.

She moved, shifting against the door, and he glanced up, his eyes meeting hers. They looked sad, his entire expression somber, tight. But then his blue gaze cleared and he smiled, standing up.

"Hello, Sophie."

Oh God, just hearing his voice made her knees weak and made her want to run to him. "Hello, Ian."

He propped his hands on the edge of his desk. "How have you been?"

Always in check, always polite at work. She much preferred him wild and unrestrained, his gaze hot, moaning when she touched him. "I've been fine. Busy."

"I've been busy as well. I was out of town on business for the past week." He came around the desk, stopped and leaned his butt against it. He crossed his arms in front of him as if waiting for a response.

She cleared her throat, nervous by his closeness. Just a few steps and she'd be right next to him, would be able to touch him. "The bar has been crazy with the heat wave still going on. Everyone wants a drink to cool themselves off."

"I've noticed the numbers have been up. I guess that's one good thing about this heat." He smiled again, but it didn't quite light up his eyes. No, really he just looked miserable.

"Did you call me to your office for a reason?"

Ian looked like he was about to say something but then he closed his eyes briefly, shaking his head. "No. I just wanted to see you."

"Oh."

"Why haven't you called me, Sophie? Or tried to see me?"

"I could ask you the same thing."

"I didn't want to push. You seemed upset when my parents stopped by and then you left without a word..."

Sophie sighed. She still felt bad about that. "I'm sorry. I didn't think you wanted me around when your family was there." More like *she* didn't want to be around when his family was there.

"I didn't mind, I want you to meet them eventually but maybe I'm rushing things..."

"Whoa, wait a minute. Rushing things? Rushing what, may I ask?"

"Well, I guess I kind of assumed we were together."

Huh? She thought he assumed they were getting together to have fun, not to have a relationship. She couldn't contain the

111

hope that rose within her at his words, though. "We've fooled around a couple of times. You just broke up with your girlfriend. I definitely didn't think we were 'together', as you say."

"You're telling me what we shared meant nothing to you."

It meant everything to her but she couldn't admit that. Didn't want him to know just how badly she wanted him, wanted something meaningful with him. All of the other men, all of the other disappointing relationships in her life, evaporated when she thought about Ian. What he did for her, how he made her feel. Treasured, appreciated, cared for. Maybe even eventually loved.

"I'm telling you I didn't think it meant anything to *you*. I thought I was your rebound relationship."

He smiled and the sight of it warmed her heart, besides other places on her body. "Sophie, if you only knew how much you consume me. Everything I see, everything I think about, talk about, I always wonder, 'How would Sophie feel?' 'What would Sophie say?' Especially after our weekend together, I've known."

"You've known what?" Her throat suddenly felt tight, overwhelmed by what he had said.

"How much I want you in my life. I wanted to give you time to know how you felt about me, but I couldn't wait anymore. I had to see you."

Ian came towards her and then she was in his arms, her face pressed against his chest. She breathed deep, his familiar spicy smell filling her nostrils, and she smiled. He buried his face in her hair.

"Do you think we could make this work?"

"What did you mean, how I felt about you?" She wished she could undress him right here, press her lips against his naked chest, run her hands all over his bare skin.

"You don't like the fact that I'm your boss. I know you're gun shy about relationships but I swear I'm not like those other men who took advantage of you." He kissed her forehead, the touch of his lips whisper soft and she melted.

Sophie had filled him in briefly on her troubled relationship past during their shut-in weekend. She'd felt comfortable letting him know, wanted him to know about it. Maybe it had been a bit of a test, but it looked like he passed.

"I can get over that if you can. As long as you don't boss me around," she teased.

Ian pulled back, watching her, his gaze smoldering. "You don't seem to mind it when I boss you around in bed."

She stood on tiptoe, pressing her lips to his for a too brief kiss. "That's different."

His hands cupped the back of her head, his mouth so close to hers his breath fanned her face. "I wish I could make love to you right here. It's been far too long since I've been with you, touched you."

"Have you ever done it in your office?" Sophie cocked a brow.

He shook his head, a wicked grin on his face. "Never."

"Then maybe we should do something about that." She kissed him again, her mouth lingering, tongue sneaking out to trace the outline of his lips. "Spontaneity is what got us in trouble in the first place."

He moaned and his mouth opened, allowing her tongue to slip inside and meet his. "I'm all for spontaneous," he said when he broke away.

"Why don't you go lock the door?" She slipped her arms around his neck and plunged her fingers into the thick hair at the back of his head. She was never going to let go of this man again.

"I will," Ian said, trying to get out of her grasp, but she wouldn't let him.

So he kissed her instead.

About the Author

After leaving the working world to become a stay at home mom/slave, Karen Erickson realized she needed to get crackin' and pursue her lifelong dream of being a published writer. A busy mother of three, she fits her precious writing time in between chasing her children, taking care of her wonderful husband and pretending she has a maid. She lives in California.

You can visit Karen at her website www.karenwritesromance.com or her blog at www.karenwritesromance.com/blog.

Look for these titles by
Karen Erickson

Now Available:

Fortune's Deception

Bad Moon Rising

Elle Kennedy

Dedication

To Lori Borrill, the best friend and critique partner a girl could have. Thanks for your advice, support and that unfailing ability to make me laugh.

Chapter One

Hailey Burke needed two things: aspirin and sex. The former could be easily attained and simply required a quick car ride to the drugstore. The latter? Well, she'd have to settle for her vibrator. Which seriously annoyed her. Considering she'd spent an entire week crying and cursing Todd for sleeping with his secretary, she felt she was owed some decent rebound sex.

This was California, for Pete's sake—where the hell were all the available, casual-sex-minded men?

Probably sleeping with their secretaries.

With a rueful sigh, Hailey slid into the driver's seat of her ancient Mazda convertible and stuck the key in the ignition. Overhead, the moon dominated the inky sky, a perfect white circle surrounded by a yellow glow that reflected off the eerily calm ocean a few dozen yards away. A full moon. She stared at it for a moment, trying to remember what it was people always said about full moons.

Something about insomnia, she recalled. And about people behaving in abnormal ways, though she wasn't sure if that was actually true.

Turning her gaze away, she flicked the ignition and reversed out of the gravel driveway of the small oceanfront cottage she shared with two girls from work. Marilee and Sam were away for the week at some ritzy Caribbean resort, probably screwing every guy who crossed their path and having that time of their life the *Dirty Dancing* soundtrack boasted about.

Then there was Hailey. Alone in Malibu. Mourning over an asshole that didn't deserve it. Horny as hell. And suffering from a headache so irritating she was driving to the pharmacy for some pills.

She let out another sigh. She really had to quit sulking. Her mother always said it gave you wrinkles. Then again, her mother was also the spokeswoman for every plastic-surgery procedure out there, so what did the woman know about wrinkles?

Hailey switched gears and headed for the twenty-four-hour drugstore off the Pacific Coast Highway. It was a little past eleven, but the summer breeze was warm. Sultry. Brushing over her bare arms and reminding her that she hadn't been touched by a man in—what? Three months? Todd always claimed to be too tired for sex. Lawyers worked hard, they got tired.

Apparently lawyers got tired from working their secretaries.

Five minutes and one aspirin later, Hailey sank back against the Mazda's torn leather seat and inhaled the salty air. She didn't want to go home just yet, so she sat in the well-lit parking lot of the plaza for a while, breathing, thinking, cursing Todd for wasting eight months of her life.

Before she could run their breakup over in her head for the millionth time, her purse started ringing. With Todd shoved back to a tiny dungeon in her brain, she fumbled for the phone and let out a breath of relief when she saw the number flashing across the screen. Austin.

"Thanks for calling me back," she chided into her cell.

"Are we not talking right now?" came his dry voice.

"I called you hours ago."

"I just got in now. The magazine had me review this new club that opened up in Santa Monica."

She leaned back in her seat again. "Was it any good?"

"Naah. But Britney Spears made an appearance, so I got a few paragraphs out of that. What are you up to?"

"Absolutely nothing. Do you want to get together?"

"Uh..."

"C'mon, don't blow me off. I need to get out of my house. I need to hang out with a friend."

"Look, you know you're always welcome at my place but—"

"Thanks, Austin! I'll be there in ten."

She clicked off the phone before he could object. So what if she was being pushy. She couldn't mope around forever, and besides, she hadn't seen Austin in weeks. He was her best male friend, probably the one normal presence in her life seeing as her mother was a Barbie doll and her roommates were sex-crazed swimsuit models. Not to mention two-timing Todd, the jerk who'd turned her life upside down the last couple months.

Maybe it wasn't sex she needed, she thought as she started the car again. Maybe what she really needed tonight was a friend.

ଛୀଓଷ

"We're no longer friends," Hailey hissed ten minutes later.

She stood in the narrow front hallway of Austin's loft, trying very hard not to poke her head into the main room and glare at the man inside. Next to her, Austin shrugged. "Hey, I tried to warn you."

"You should've tried harder. I'd never have come if I knew he was here."

He was Zack Creighton. Zack, the guy who worked out at the same gym as Todd. The guy who'd probably known all about Todd's adulterous ways and hadn't said one word to her. Zack, the guy who'd fucked both of her roommates, never to be seen again.

She didn't like Zack.

Clutching the strap of her purse, she edged toward the door, the headache she'd just gotten rid of returning full force. Screw friendship. If she left now she could make it home in time for the last half of *The Tonight Show*, and maybe enjoy a nice vibrator-induced orgasm afterwards.

"C'mon, he's not so bad," Austin said quietly, his blue eyes softening. "You two just got off on the wrong foot."

She stuck out her chin. "He broke my roommate's heart."

"Which roommate?" Austin flashed an impish grin.

Hailey didn't return the grin. She'd had to deal with one sleazy, arrogant man this month and she wasn't in the mood to spend her night with another. Zack Creighton annoyed her. His bad-boy persona annoyed her. And right now, she wasn't up for any more annoyances mucking up her life.

"What, you're not going to come in and say hello?" came a mocking voice.

Hailey glared at Austin, who simply shrugged again. "You can't ignore him now," he pointed out.

Green eyes narrowing, Hailey stepped back into the doorway and peered into the main room. And there he was. Sitting on Austin's tattered leather couch, one denim-clad leg slung over the other, his seductive black eyes taunting her from across the loft.

"Hello, Zack," she called coolly, crossing her arms over her chest.

The corner of his wide mouth lifted. "Don't sound so enthusiastic, babe."

She moved out of Zack Creighton's line of sight. "He called me babe," she grumbled. "I'm leaving."

Austin chuckled, then curled his fingers over her arm. "Stay and have a beer."

"Austin."

"One beer." He swept his gaze over her face, his expression wry. "Come on, you look like you need it."

Chapter Two

"Full moon," Zack remarked, glancing out the window as he sipped the cold beer Austin handed him. He turned to the curvy redhead sulking in the armchair next to the couch. "You know what they say about full moons, don't you, Hailey?"

Her lush red lips tightened. "What do they say, Zack?"

"That full moons make people act crazy."

She arched a brow. "Gotta be some truth to that, seeing as I'm spending the evening in your company."

He swallowed back a laugh. Damn, she really didn't like him, did she? Zack had sensed Hailey's dislike for him the moment they met, though he wasn't sure he blamed her considering the circumstances in which they'd been introduced. It had been seven o'clock in the morning, and a sleepy-eyed Hailey, dark red hair all tousled from slumber, had walked into the kitchen to find her roommate Marilee on her knees, er, servicing him.

Not the most comfortable of meetings, to say the least.

But hell, the way Hailey had balked and rushed out of the room...it was like she'd never seen a guy getting a blow job before.

Maybe he was the asshole Hailey thought he was. Maybe he'd dated her roommates and broken it off with both. But

Marilee and Sam had known exactly what they were getting into when they got involved with him. He hadn't lied, or cheated or manipulated the women in any way. In fact, he highly doubted either one had cried or moaned over the breakups. Swimsuit models didn't sleep with photographers hoping for a long-lasting relationship, they did it to get ahead.

Not that Hailey would understand. She only worked as an assistant at the modeling agency, not a model like the women she shared a house with.

Though with her gorgeous face and mouth-watering curves, Hailey Burke could definitely give her roommates a run for their money.

"You know," Austin piped up, "maybe this full moon could do some good. Maybe the two of you will stop bitching at one another."

"Not likely," Hailey said under her breath.

Zack cast her a grin. "C'mon, babe, you don't find me the least bit appealing ?"

"Nope." Although she fixed her gaze on the television, she didn't seem too interested in the mindless sitcom flashing across the screen.

Zack wasn't fazed by the way she ignored him. He was used to it by now. Funny how wherever he went, Hailey seemed to pop up. He'd first met her through her roommates, but once both those brief romances fizzled he'd figured he'd never see her again. Until he'd learned that she was good friends with Austin, who worked at the magazine Zack freelanced for every now and then. Of course, Hailey made sure to visit her good friend Austin whenever Zack wasn't around, but even then their paths kept crossing. She'd started dating his workout buddy. Then it turned out they visited the same dry cleaner, liked the same restaurants, went to the same movies.

Fate kept throwing Hailey Burke right back in his path, whether or not she wanted to be there.

Too damn bad for her. For him, her constant appearances in his life amused him.

Not to mention strengthened that unbelievably foolish urge to fuck her.

"So how's your sister?" Hailey asked Austin, continuing to ignore him.

"Gracie's fine. She's back with Steve."

"Slimy Steve?" Hailey made a face.

"The one and only."

"God, the sex must be really, really good if she took him back again. She hates that guy."

A pained expression crossed Austin's face. "As much as it revolts me to think of my sister having sex with anyone, you probably have a point. Gracie has admitted numerous times that she doesn't like the guy."

"Like I said, really good sex."

Zack cocked his head. "So you think it's perfectly acceptable to sleep with someone you don't like?"

Hailey flashed him a sweet smile and tossed her silky red hair over her shoulder. "Sure. Women go to bed with you all the time and I can't see why any of them would like you."

Ouch.

Normally he'd have a snappy comeback ready to go but he came up empty-handed. Besides, Hailey was actually speaking to him, and *looking* at him while she did, so he had no inclination to rock the boat.

"What about you, babe?" he asked, curious. "Would you have sex with a man you didn't like?"

She licked her bottom lip. He fought the urge to march over to the armchair and lick that lip with his own tongue.

"It depends," she finally replied.

"On what?"

"On whether the attraction is stronger than the hatred."

"So if you're hot enough for the guy you'll fuck him regardless of how you feel about him?"

"Again, it depends."

Their gazes collided and something in the air shifted. Oh man. Was that a glimmer of arousal he saw in those forest green eyes? Sitting in the darkness of the loft it was hard to tell, but the faint moonlight streaming in from the window blinds provided just enough light to confirm it. Arousal.

Imperceptible, but there.

The full moon. That had to be it.

Hailey shifted in her chair and fought the spark of desire heating her thighs. No way was she attracted to Zack Creighton. No way in hell.

It was the moon. And maybe there was something in the aspirin too. Why else would she be imagining him naked right now?

And boy, it wasn't hard to conjure up a nude image of Zack. She'd already seen him naked. Once. In her kitchen, while Marilee licked his rock-hard cock.

The memory should've evoked some sense of revulsion, but all it did was make her clit ache.

"Hey, we're getting somewhere," Austin declared, looking pleased as punch. "You two are having an actual conversation."

When she glanced over she didn't miss the flush on Austin's cheeks and that slightly glazed look in his eyes. "Are you drunk?"

"Buzzed. I only had a few drinks at the club."

She pointed to the two empty beer bottles on the splintered oak coffee table. "And two more here."

"Hailey, it's Friday night. I'm allowed to drink."

He was right. She didn't know why she'd turned mother hen on him all of a sudden. Austin was thirty years old; he had every right to drink however much he wanted. In fact, she really ought to follow his lead. She'd been so stressed out lately. All the problems with Todd. Her hectic work schedule.

Her roommates always teased her about needing to lighten up, but she rarely ever listened. Mari and Sam, their jobs were in no way as demanding as hers. They posed for pictures in their bikinis. Hailey was the one who helped the head of the agency schedule the shoots, talked to the photographers, made sure all the girls got paid. Tons of irksome, menial tasks that kept her busy. And prevented her from lightening up.

But maybe it was time to unwind. Just a little. It was summer, after all. Summer meant lazy days and hot, endless nights. Not only that, but it was the weekend. No work. No responsibilities.

It really wouldn't kill her to have some fun.

Even if it meant having fun with Zack Creighton.

With a sigh, she polished off the rest of her beer and got to her feet. "You guys want anything from the fridge?"

Both men requested beers, so Hailey made her way across the spacious loft toward the open-concept kitchenette. She bent down in front of the mini fridge and grabbed three longnecks from the top shelf, then headed back to the main living area and tossed each guy a drink.

Popping off the lid, she raised the bottle to her lips and drank in the chilled, bitter liquid. It felt nice as it slid down her throat. Her body cooled, then warmed again as the balmy breeze drifting in from the open window met her bare shoulders. Her tank top clung to her skin a little, not just from the warm air but from the alcohol slithering its way through her veins.

Although she tried not to, she glanced over at Zack again. His black T-shirt stretched across his chest, emphasizing the defined ripples of his stomach, and her mouth grew dry as she imagined walking over there and sliding her hands underneath the cotton material, running her fingers over all that hard muscle.

He caught her staring, and one dark brow lifted. He looked amused. "See anything you like?" he asked in a sandpaper-rough voice.

A flurry of shivers danced up her spine. She banished them away. "I thought we already established that I don't like much about you, Zack."

"And yet you're attracted to me."

Her mouth opened but nothing came out.

"So is this the situation you were describing?" He uncrossed his legs and leaned forward, his rugged features creasing with amusement. "Being attracted to someone you hate?"

"I'm not attracted to you," she lied.

It shocked her that she even *had* to lie. Twenty minutes ago she would've laughed at the thought of being attracted to Zack. Twenty minutes ago, however, she hadn't had two beers in her system. She wasn't drunk by any means but still...

It was the alcohol. That's why her head felt a little light, and her body was humming with sexual awareness.

One aspirin and two beers. Obviously when you put them together you got a weird, potent reaction that made you want to do stupid things. Like have sex with Zack Creighton.

Might as well throw the full moon in there too. Maybe it really was some phenomena that made people feel a little nuts.

"Come over here and prove it," Zack challenged from his perch on the sofa.

"Excuse me?"

"You heard me."

"What exactly do I need to prove?" Her voice came out as a squeak. Damn it, she was *not* allowed to squeak in front of this jerk of a man.

"That you don't find me attractive." He shrugged, causing a few strands of unruly dark brown hair to fall onto his forehead. "Kiss me. Touch me. Do whatever you want, sweetheart. Just prove that the attraction isn't there."

She looked over to Austin for help, but her friend's eyes were even more glazed than they'd been before. God, why had she brought him another beer? Austin was supposed to be her ally. He was supposed to make Zack back off and be that normal presence in her life.

So why was he just grinning at her?

"He's got a point," Austin said. "You can't tell a man you don't want him without providing some kind of proof."

"And my word isn't enough?" she grumbled.

"No," both males said in unison.

Before she could argue, the cordless phone on the coffee table began to ring.

Leaning forward, Austin grabbed it. "Hello?" He paused, and a slow smile tugged at his mouth. "Now? I'm afraid I've had a bit to drink. No driving for me tonight, honey." Another pause. The smile widened. "You're outside?"

He hung up a few moments later and stumbled to his feet. "You two feel free to stay as long as you like." He glanced at the beer in Hailey's hand. "In fact, spend the night, Hails. I don't want you driving home."

Her jaw fell open. "Where are you going?"

"Denise is waiting in her car outside."

"Who on earth is Denise?"

Austin grinned. "Just a lady friend."

"Fuck buddy, he means," Zack spoke up, rolling his dark eyes.

Hailey stood and trailed Austin to the door. He shoved his keys in the front pocket of his khakis, plunked his cell phone in the other one and reached for the doorknob. She intercepted his hand. "You can't leave," she hissed.

"Oh, don't take it to heart. I'm buzzed and I'm about to get laid. Try to be happy for me."

She frowned. "You can't leave me here with Zack."

"You two seem to be getting along."

"He's flirting with me."

"So?"

"So I don't like it."

Austin patted her upper arm. "Sure you do."

With another grin, he slid out the door, leaving her standing in the hallway in disbelief. She swallowed, trying to figure out what to do next. Austin was right. She really shouldn't drive home, not when she was feeling this light-headed. Normally she'd have no problem crashing on her friend's couch, but tonight wasn't normal. Tonight Zack was here, and tonight her traitorous body was reacting to Zack in a way it never had before.

She sagged against the wall. If she went back in there, Zack would start flirting with her again. And God help her, but she wasn't sure she could fight off his advances.

Or that she even wanted to.

Chapter Three

"I'm not going to bite you," Zack called from the main room.

She swallowed again. Harder this time.

Back straight, she reentered the room. Zack's voice stopped her before she could sink back into the armchair. "Sit next to me."

She moved over and sat on the couch. The couch that suddenly seemed to shrink. He was too close to her. She could feel his body heat. Smell the intoxicating scent of his aftershave.

She turned her head, just a fraction of an inch, and saw fire burning in his dark eyes.

"Stop looking at me like that," she murmured.

"Like what?"

"Like you're imagining me without my clothes on."

"I *am* imagining you without your clothes on."

"Well, stop it."

"I'm afraid I don't really want to."

She shot him a glare, but that only made the scorching flames in his gaze deepen. Before she could blink, he slid closer and placed one big hand directly on her thigh. The warmth of his hand seared right through the thin material of her Capris.

Her nipples instantly hardened and poked against her tank top. Damn it. Why hadn't she worn a bra?

"Hailey," Zack said.

"Yes?"

"Why exactly don't you like me?"

Her jaw tensed. "You know why."

"You think I'm too much of a ladies' man."

"Yep."

"You think I'm arrogant."

"Yep."

"Yet I still manage to turn you on."

"No," she lied.

He gave a knowing glance before fixing his gaze on her breasts. "Your nipples are hard."

"I'm cold."

"It's ninety degrees." He licked his lips in a way that should've been sleazy but instead looked pretty damn enticing. "What would you do if I put my hands underneath your shirt? Would you stop me?"

Her clit swelled as a rush of liquid heat pooled in her panties.

"I don't think you would," he continued, moving even closer. He dragged his palm up her thigh, over her navel, until it was inches away from her breasts. "I think you'd beg me to keep going."

"Your arrogance astounds me," she squeezed out.

"Deny it all you want, but we both know what's running through that pretty red head of yours right now."

"Oh, please enlighten me." It was a miracle she managed to keep her voice calm. Inside, she was a trembling mess, hot, needy, so painfully aroused it hurt to talk.

"You're thinking about all the things I could do to your body. With my hands and my tongue." He dipped his head and bit her earlobe. "And my teeth."

A jolt of excitement shot from her ear, to her breasts and straight down to her pussy. Somehow she was wetter than she'd ever been.

"Let's not be coy, Hailey. Admit you want me."

Their eyes locked and something inside her caved. "Fine. So maybe I do. Just a bit. But I still don't like you," she added.

"Didn't we just establish liking each other had nothing to do with wanting each other?"

Had they established that? He seemed to think so. She was beginning to think it too, what with her hard nipples and damp panties.

The window blinds rustled as another gust of hot air drifted into the room. She shifted in her seat, agitated, her lower body tight with anticipation. Aw hell. Would it really be so bad, going to bed with this man? He was deliciously attractive, with his dark, smoldering eyes and that strong jaw covered with stubble and those wicked lips she couldn't help but want to kiss. The moonlight brought out the roughness of his features, making him appear dangerous. And totally sexy.

She found herself leaning closer to him, angling her chin so that their lips were millimeters away. His warm breath fanned against her, minty, with just the slightest scent of alcohol. She knew he wasn't drunk; he'd only taken two sips of the beer she'd brought him. Which meant that Zack Creighton, in all his sober, magnificent glory, wanted to have sex with her.

And God help her, but the feeling was mutual.

"One night," she blurted out.

He tilted his head. "Huh?"

"I don't want to get involved with you." She inhaled, hoping to bring some much-needed oxygen to her lungs. "This will just be a one-night thing."

"Whatever you say." He winked. He actually *winked.*

Before she could weasel a promise out of him that this wouldn't go beyond one night, he kissed her.

Mouth crushing over hers. Lips rubbing against hers. Hot, wet tongue thrusting inside her mouth without invitation. Hands down it was the most erotic kiss she'd ever had. Deep and greedy, fast and passionate.

Zack's stubble chafed her chin, the rough sensation making her moan against his lips.

God, his mouth felt nice.

Really nice.

Flicking his tongue over hers, he shoved his hand under her shirt and palmed one breast, rubbing her nipple with the pad of his thumb. Then, to her dismay, he broke the kiss.

"Why are you stopping?" she complained.

"I'm not." Without another word, he lifted the tank top right over her head and tossed it aside. A second later, he lowered his head and covered her breast with his mouth.

A gasp tore out of her throat. Now she understood the reason for the incessant moaning that had come out of Mari's bedroom when she'd dated Zack. The man's tongue was...lethal. Skilled. He licked the underside of one breast and kissed his way up to her nipple, rubbing his lips against it and then sucking it hard into his mouth.

It was a tongue that refused to stop. Licking, swirling, gliding down to her navel, and circling her bellybutton. And

136

soon his hands came into play once more. They tugged at the zipper of her Capris and slid it down with a metallic hiss. He peeled the pants off her tanned legs, threw them aside and dropped to his knees in front of her.

"What do you want, Hailey?"

His voice teased her, mocked her. It was too confident, too heavy with sexual promise, but she couldn't muster enough indignation to respond with. Truth was, his confidence excited her.

"You know what I want," she returned, feeling bold as she widened her legs.

He reached out and brushed his fingers over the damp crotch of her black bikini panties. "You want me to stroke you?"

"Uh-huh," she breathed.

"Suck on your clit?"

"Mmm-hmmm."

"Make you come?"

"God, yes."

She swallowed and tried not to cry out. Her body ached, actually ached for this man. He continued to kneel there, planting featherlight caresses on her pussy, and to make it worse, he was still fully dressed! Here she was, her breasts bare, her nipples painfully hard, her panties practically begging to be flung aside, and Zack was still in jeans and a T-shirt and looking unhurried to remove them.

"I'm curious, sweetheart," he said, stroking her with one hand. "Do you come fast or slow?"

"Huh?" She tried to focus but it was difficult seeing as his fingers kept pressing against her clit that way.

"If I took these panties off and pressed my tongue between your legs, would you come right away?" He shot her a small grin. "Or are you the type who prolongs the pleasure and tries to control your orgasm?" He emphasized his last word by rubbing lazy circles over her clit.

"I come fast, Zack," she choked out.

He nodded. "Not tonight, Hailey."

He hooked his fingers under the waistband of her panties and pulled the material to her ankles, then eased her legs open. Licking his bottom lip, he stared at her for a moment, and only his sharp intake of breath betrayed his cool, take-charge composure.

"Like what you see?" she found herself taunting.

"Very much."

She gestured to his clothes with one trembling hand. "When do I get to see you?"

"Later."

Ever so leisurely, he slid closer and lowered his head to her throbbing center. Her body tensed, waiting, anticipating, and finally, finally his tongue darted out and touched her swollen clit. She shivered. He licked again. She shuddered.

"More," she pleaded.

He ignored her and began tracing her labia with the tip of his tongue. He licked a wet line down her slit, then stole the breath right out of her lungs by shoving his tongue deep inside her pussy.

"Oh God," she gasped.

And so it continued. Languid torturous licks and soft, barely there kisses, and then he'd switch it up and tongue her hard. Slide a finger inside only to withdraw it the second her inner muscles clamped over it. He was an evil man. Every time she got close he stopped. Sometimes he chuckled at her agitated whimpers, other times he ignored them altogether. He made her believe he'd allow her to climax, stroking her faster, sucking her harder, but then slowing the pace before she could topple over the edge.

It was a seesaw. Pleasure rising, pleasure climbing, pleasure dropping back to a throbbing ache that Zack refused to tend to.

"Please," she whispered.

"No."

The seesaw continued its up-and-down routine. She was close, so close...and then she wasn't. Close, far, close, far.

Hailey didn't know how much time had passed, how long Zack knelt there between her legs, torturing her into oblivion, and when he finally pressed his mouth against her clit and shoved two fingers inside her she didn't even see the orgasm coming.

Her body exploded. A tsunami of ecstasy slammed into her, so intense it almost hurt. And the moonlight bathing the room only heightened her fierce reaction, teasing her senses, shining in Zack's dark hair in a way that made him appear like an apparition, a ghostly, sexy vision between her thighs. It was all too much. She trembled violently, moan after moan slipping out of her mouth and filling the unlit loft.

With one final brush of his tongue, Zack straightened his shoulders and leaned back. "Get up," he said in a rough voice.

The taste of honey and vanilla lingered in Zack's mouth as he lifted a naked Hailey to her feet and led her toward the double bed on the other side of the room. His gaze kept darting to her delectable curves. Her firm ass. Those perky breasts, nipples hard and skin reddened from his day-old beard scraping against it.

He hadn't planned on sleeping with her tonight. Hell, how could he? He'd come over here to have some drinks with an old friend, nothing more. And yet the moment Hailey walked in with her clingy tank top and tight pants he'd reacted to her.

He'd always reacted to her.

Her sass. Her fiery personality. The way she never backed down from a challenge.

She might not like him very much, but he liked her. Yes, he antagonized her every chance he got, but for no other reason than to ruffle a few of her feathers. Zack wasn't used to women not liking him, avoiding him and rebuffing his advances. Hailey did all those things, yet tonight she'd somehow dropped her guard. Tonight she'd responded to his presence, to his kisses, and he planned on making sure she didn't walk away from him so easily this time.

She said she wanted this to be a one-night stand but after watching her come apart on the sofa he had no intention of leaving it as that.

Hailey lowered herself onto the bed, stretching out on the blue bedspread and eyeing him expectantly. He didn't join her, not yet. Instead, he pushed his zipper down and shucked his jeans and boxers, then pulled his T-shirt over his head and dropped it on the hardwood floor.

It pleased him the way Hailey's eyes widened.

His cock twitched, hardening even more—which seemed impossible. He'd never had a hard-on like this before. It almost troubled him, how turned on he was.

"What are you waiting for?" Hailey grumbled.

Her green eyes were dark with sex and impatience, and though he would've enjoyed teasing her, testing her self-control by having her lie there in wait, his body wouldn't allow it. He grabbed a condom from his wallet and rolled it onto his shaft, then lowered his body next to hers. Once more he tried slowing the pace, running one hand up her thighs, lightly stroking her hot sex while his other hand slid up to cup a breast.

A strangled breath exited her lush mouth. "For God's sake, Zack. Fuck me."

What man could deny a request like that?

Shifting over, he moved between her firm, tanned thighs and touched her opening with his index finger, tormenting her just a bit longer. When she gave a desperate little whimper, he replaced the finger with his cock and eased his tip into her, then chuckled as she let out a mumbled expletive. "More," she ordered.

"This much more?" He pushed in another inch.

"No, *this* much more." Before he could blink, she dug her hands into his ass and drew him deeper inside her.

A red haze clouded his vision, his entire body throbbing at the way her tight wetness surrounded his dick. "Jesus," he hissed out.

With Hailey's fingernails drawing half circles on his butt, he started to move. Thrusting forward so his entire length was encased in her velvet heat, then withdrawing fully as they both groaned.

The slow pace didn't last. Before long, he was pumping furiously, driving into her over and over again as white-hot pleasure rose inside his body like a plane ascending in takeoff.

"You realize I'm..." Hailey gasped, "about to..." she moaned, "come again."

And come she did. Her pussy tightened around his cock at the same time she let out a sexy cry that made his pulse drum in his ears. He tried to hold off, tried to enjoy the feel of her shuddering beneath him, groaning in his ear as she wrapped her arms around him and sucked on his neck. Resisting was futile. He came a second later, a violent, bone-numbing release that had him cursing and grunting loudly. Ten minutes later, the waves of pleasure finally ebbed.

Ten minutes after that, he fucked her again.

Chapter Four

Hailey snuck out of Austin's loft at the crack of dawn without so much as planting a kiss on Zack's sleeping, stubble-covered face. Call her callous, call her a coward, but she couldn't fight the overwhelming urge to get away from him. As fast as she humanly could.

Outside Austin's small building, the air was as warm as it had been the night before, only instead of that potent, ethereal moonlight, the sun was shining. Not one cloud tainted the clear blue sky, and yards away the beach already boasted a few early-morning joggers, their sneakers leaving fresh footsteps over the stretch of clean sand, the ocean peaceful and the waves quiet.

A seagull squawked in the distance, prompting Hailey to snap out of her melancholy scrutiny of her surroundings. She made a beeline for her car, flopped inside and started the engine. Her right foot shook as she stepped on the gas pedal.

Her body still ached from Zack's erotic assault.

What had gotten into her last night? Was it the full moon, the two beers she'd consumed? What had inspired her to go to bed with a man she didn't even like?

Not that the sex had been bad. Oh no, it had been great. Hot. Mind-blowing.

In fact, if she were honest, she'd admit it was the best goddamn sex of her life.

She drove fast, willing to risk a speeding ticket if it meant putting Zack Creighton and his talented hands and wicked tongue far behind her. She didn't want to think about him, or his cock, or the way he'd set her entire body on fire. If she allowed herself to relive it, she feared she'd turn the car around and hop back into bed with him.

಄ೲ

Zack had barely zipped up his pants when Austin entered the loft with the swagger of a man who'd gotten laid and the grin of a man who'd gotten laid good. The smile on Austin's face faded, however, the second he spotted Zack standing in front of his bed, clad in nothing but jeans.

Austin instantly moved his head from side to side, scanning the brightly lit apartment. "Where is she?"

"Gone." One word, punctuated by a bitter frown.

Never had a woman walked out on him after a night of mind-blowing sex. *He* was usually the one who did the walking, and it had seriously pissed him off to wake up and find Hailey AWOL.

Austin held up his hand in a warning gesture. "Don't tell me you slept with her."

"Okay, I won't tell you." He bent down and picked up the T-shirt he'd tossed on the floor. Slipping it on, he met his friend's disapproving gaze and shrugged. "For Christ's sake, man, it was consensual."

"She was drunk and you took advantage."

"She was not drunk, and trust me, Hailey wasn't telling me to stop."

Austin tightened his lips and strode toward him. "She's a good woman, and a good friend, Creighton. What the hell made you decide to mess around with her?"

Zack paused. Though he'd been asking himself the same question since he'd woken up, the answer still eluded him. He'd always been attracted to Hailey Burke, yeah, but he'd never made a move because truth was, she really didn't seem to like him. At first he'd told himself it was a playing-hard-to-get kind of dislike, but after a year of running into Hailey through mutual acquaintances and at random places, he'd realized the woman wasn't playing games.

And he knew all about games in his line of work. As a freelance photographer for some of the top fashion magazines in the country, he constantly encountered women who liked to toy with him, models who flirted shamelessly in hopes of landing a shoot with him. He could always tell the difference between a woman who was being coy and one who flat-out detested him.

Sadly, Hailey was the latter.

Well, too fucking bad for her. Last night proved they had chemistry. Hot, combustible chemistry that he'd never shared with any other female.

Could he really ignore that kind of chemistry?

"I like her," he told his friend.

Austin raised one dark blond eyebrow. "Since when?"

"Since always." He blew out an exasperated breath. "She's the one who has a problem with me, not the other way around."

With a dubious expression, Austin said, "You're being straight with me?"

"I sure as hell am."

"So she wasn't just a one-night stand for you?"

"Not by a long shot."

A faint smile crossed Austin's face. "Does Hailey know that?"

"Not yet. But I intend to let her know."

℘)℘

Although Zack had called the cottage five times since she'd snuck out of the loft earlier in the morning, Hailey didn't pick up the phone. She'd seen his number on the Caller ID and let the calls go to the machine, hoping sooner or later Zack would give up and leave her alone. She didn't want to talk to him. Again, it was taking the coward's way out, but she didn't care. What happened between her and Zack last night was too...confusing.

Yep, she was thoroughly confused.

For Hailey, caution and relationships went hand in hand. She'd never been impulsive when it came to dating, and certainly never reckless about sex, so her actions last night made no sense to her. It was as if an external, erotic force had taken over her body and sent her straight into Zack's arms. Casual sex... It wasn't like her to indulge in something so crazy. Her roommates wouldn't hesitate indulging, but that's why Mari and Sam were models and Hailey was an executive assistant. She was too rational, too careful-minded to be wild.

Zack, on the other hand, had written the book on wild. At the modeling agency, Hailey had heard plenty of rumors—and witnessed most of them firsthand—about the sexy, spontaneous photographer. His work truly was good, but she knew the reason most models liked working with Zack Creighton had more to do with his flirtatious bad-boy ways than his photographic talent.

Bottom line—he wasn't her type. And that's precisely why she didn't answer the phone when he called, and why she deleted his messages from her answering machine. Last night she'd told him she didn't want more than one night with him, and she'd meant it. Didn't matter how phenomenal the sex had been—men like Zack weren't cut out for relationships, at least in her humble opinion. So it had, *had* to end at one night.

Unfortunately, Zack didn't agree. She realized this later in the evening when she opened her door and found the dark-haired bad boy standing on her doorstep.

"You were avoiding my calls," he said with a disapproving frown.

"I was busy," she lied.

Without waiting for an invitation inside, Zack strode into the cottage and dropped his car keys on the hall table. She watched openmouthed as he marched into the living room and flopped down on the plush white couch.

"I want to take you on a date," he announced, clasping his hands on his lap.

She laughed. "No you don't. You just want to have sex with me again."

He met her gaze, eyes narrowed. "That too. But I'm serious about the date."

"Well, forget it." She crossed her arms over her chest. "I told you, I don't want to get involved."

"You got involved with Todd, and he's ten times the sleaze you think I am." He imitated her by crossing his arms over his broad chest. "And I'm no sleaze, Hailey. In fact, you're so wrong about me it's almost laughable."

"I'm wrong about you, huh?"

"You sure are."

"Then you didn't sleep with *both* my roommates?"

"I did. Not at the same time, though."

"And you don't get involved with the other models you photograph?"

"Not as many as you think, sweetheart." He set his strong jaw, then raked one hand through his hair. "Let's get a few things straight, Hailey. I like sex, sure—what man doesn't? But I don't gallivant around sticking my dick in anything that moves. I've had one serious relationship. It ended. Since then I've been playing the field, but there's no crime in that."

He leaned forward, his features softening. "I take my work seriously. I'm *proud* of my work. So is my family, for that matter. My parents have all the covers I've shot framed and hanging over their fireplace. Every Sunday I go over to their house and play chess with my father. Then I help my mother cook dinner." Sarcasm dripped from his tone. "How sleazy does that sound?"

Her resolve faltered. She didn't miss the fondness in his voice when he mentioned his parents or the pride he felt over his work. In a split second, he'd transformed from a one-dimensional womanizer to a three-dimensional man with a family and ambitions. It freaked her out a little.

"So come on, Hailey, let me take you out to dinner."

She swallowed. "You don't even like me."

He chuckled, and the husky sound made her shiver. "I've liked you from the moment I met you."

"You have?" She tried to keep her jaw up where it belonged.

"Oh yeah." Without breaking their gaze, he got to his feet and moved toward her. "I like the way you challenge me, the way you make me laugh, the way your cheeks get all flushed when you're pissed off. And"—he reached out and touched her lips—"I like the way you felt in my arms last night."

"Oh,"

Her mouth suddenly grew dry while her mind worked overtime trying to figure out whether he meant everything he'd just said. It was hard to think, though, with him standing so close to her, with his spicy, male scent drifting into her nostrils. Fighting the urge to kiss him, she stepped back and rubbed her forehead.

"I need some air." She swallowed again. "Do you want to walk on the beach with me?"

Chapter Five

Baby steps. She hadn't agreed to a date with him yet, but Zack would take what he could get. Hands shoved in the pockets of his khakis, he walked alongside Hailey on the warm sand, breathing in the salty summer air. He hadn't lied back there. He really did like the redhead next to him. He just wished Hailey would drop all the unfounded misconceptions she'd formed about him and give him a chance to prove he wasn't the badass she thought he was.

Deciding to take a chance, he reached out for her hand. For a moment she didn't respond, but then she twined her fingers with his and continued walking.

The beach was surprisingly deserted. Not a person in sight. And the ocean was calm, the tide barely making a sound as it crept onto the shore before retreating again.

They stopped in a secluded spot, where a set of large boulders dug into the sand and a thick palm cast a shadow over them. With a sigh, Hailey turned to face him, her green eyes swimming with something he couldn't decipher. Confusion maybe. And definitely a flicker of desire.

Before he could blink, she pressed her body against his and kissed him.

Her lips were hot and pliant, her tongue hesitant as it darted out and touched his lower lip. He returned the kiss, but didn't deepen it, just let Hailey take the lead as he rested his hands on her slim waist.

"This is crazy," she whispered into his mouth. She pulled back, and again her eyes glittered with a mixture of uncertainty and arousal. "I've gone crazy."

"Because you like kissing me?"

She nodded. "Not to mention the fact that I can't stop thinking about taking your pants off."

Instant erection. Fighting back a groan, Zack shifted, willing his cock to go down. If he was going to convince Hailey to go out with him, he couldn't come off as a horny Neanderthal.

Unfortunately, she refused to allow him his honor.

With a mischievous smile, she lowered her hand and cupped him through the khaki material. His cock twitched against her palm.

"What are you doing?" he said in a low voice.

"God, I don't know." She rubbed his hard ridge. "Like I said, I think I've gone crazy."

They might have been standing under the shadow of a palm, and slightly shielded from view by the boulders beside them, but Zack knew any passerby would be able to see what Hailey was doing to him.

"We should go back to the cottage," he murmured.

"Not yet."

She squeezed his crotch. Then, to his shock, she reached for his waist and unbuttoned his pants. His zipper soon slid down.

He intercepted her hand. "Hailey..."

"Oh come on," she teased. "Don't tell me you actually want me to stop."

151

"We're out in the open."

"So?"

She tugged on his waistband and pulled down his pants and boxers, just low enough that his cock jutted out.

"Can I tell you something?" she asked.

He grunted as she touched the tip of his dick with her index finger. "Mmm-hmmm?"

"I've wanted to do this to you since the day I walked into the kitchen and found you and Marilee together." She met his gaze with a slight flush on her cheeks. "I know, it sounds perverted, and to be honest, I never even admitted it to myself until now. But I think I was jealous. Of Mari. I wanted to be the one on my knees, sucking you off."

His penis went hard as granite. He would've never pegged Hailey as the dirty-talk kind of woman. He liked it.

What she did next, he liked even more.

Sliding down to her knees, she licked the sensitive underside of his shaft, then took his entire length into her wet mouth.

Zack almost came on the spot. It was too much, glancing down and seeing Hailey's full lips wrapped around his cock. Too much, feeling her hot tongue circling his tip, sucking the drop of moisture that had pooled there.

A few yards away, the waves grew louder, matching the turbulent arousal swirling through his body. At each crash of the water against the shore, his pleasure heightened.

Screw being in public. With Hailey licking and sucking him, he couldn't help but forget his surroundings. Reaching down, he tangled his fingers in her red hair and thrust into her mouth, enjoying the soft moan that exited her delicate throat. She quickened her pace, moving one hand over to cup his balls, kneading and tugging until he thought his legs would buckle under him.

"Jesus, Hailey, that feels... You're so..." he choked out, unable to formulate coherent sentences.

He leaned against one of the boulders and closed his eyes, losing himself in the sensations her mouth and tongue created inside him.

The pleasure became too much to bear. With a low groan, he came. Hard. Fast. Pouring his seed into her mouth and then releasing a ragged moan when he felt her swallow every drop.

His knees shook as he tried to recover from the explosive release, and Hailey continued to kiss his cock until finally he hauled her to her feet and forced her to stop. "You're going to kill me," he muttered into her ear, planting a kiss on the top of her head.

She gave a throaty laugh. "That was the plan."

With shaky hands, he pulled up his pants. "It was a very good plan."

She laughed again. "Come on, let's go back to the house. You could show me just how much you want that date of yours."

"Now *that's* a plan."

ॐ

The sex they had at her house, in her bed, was not as rough or exciting as it had been the night before, but it was just as passionate and more than satisfying. Afterwards, Hailey rested her head on Zack's chest, enjoying the masculine scent of him and the hard muscle pressing against her cheek. She couldn't remember the last time she'd felt so at ease with a man, lying in bed after sex, not needing to fill the silence that had fallen over the bedroom.

Todd had always chattered after they made love, using mindless snippets of conversation to keep his distance. He'd never let her get too close, and now, after learning about his affair with his secretary, she knew why. Todd had never loved her, he'd never looked forward to a future between the two of them like she had.

Not that she was planning a future with Zack.

She just liked the level of comfort between them, that's all.

"How come you never went into modeling?" His rough voice broke the silence, sounding more like a curious question than a need to ruin the quiet moment.

"I don't like it. Mari forced me to take some headshots once, but I was never comfortable in front of the camera. I prefer the behind-the-scenes stuff." She smiled wryly.

"So you want to be an assistant to a modeling agent for the rest of your life?"

"For now, yeah, not for the rest of my life. Once I save up more money, I want to..." Her voice drifted.

"You want to what?"

"Start an event-planning business," she sighed.

"Why do you sound so ashamed of it?" he asked with a laugh.

"I'm not ashamed. It's just...a lot of people don't take party planning seriously. They think it's frivolous work."

"Hey, if a bunch of rich folks want to pay you to plan their shindigs, who am I to judge? I think you'd be good at it."

She twisted her head to meet his dark-eyed gaze. "You do?"

"Sure. You're very...organized."

"You say it like an insult."

"I don't mean it as one. I've always thought you were detail oriented." He chuckled. "And stubborn. And a total pain in the ass most of the time."

"Funny, I thought the same things about you."

"Thought? As in you've realized your mistake and want me to take you on a date?"

Damn it. Why did he have to bring that up again? It was absurd, really. She'd already had sex with the man—why did the thought of having dinner with him make her apprehensive?

"I'm still thinking about the date thing," she finally said.

"Okay." He sounded disappointed.

"Like I said before, I'm not sure I want to get involved."

"With anyone, or is it just me?" he asked in a flat voice.

She didn't answer. Fortunately, he didn't pressure her to continue. Instead, he threaded his fingers through her hair and tilted her head so that he could kiss her. She kissed him back.

Sooner or later she'd need to give him an answer. Right now, however, she didn't want to think about anything other than the feel of his delicious mouth against hers.

Chapter Six

As it turned out, Hailey never ended up agreeing to or rejecting Zack's date invitation. Her workweek started with full force, bringing with it numerous headaches, a slew of problems at the agency and the return of her drop-dead-gorgeous, sex-crazed roommates.

Dealing with work problems was a piece of cake.

Telling Mari and Sam about Zack was not.

Every Wednesday night the three of them gathered around the television to watch *Lost*, and though it was the summer and the show was on hiatus, that didn't stop their routine. As a *Lost* rerun flashed across the plasma screen, Hailey polished off the homemade margarita Sam had whipped up and decided there was no point prolonging the inevitable.

Taking a breath, she said, "I slept with Zack."

Marilee, of course, was the first to respond. She shoved a wayward blonde curl out of her eyes and fixed Hailey with a perplexed look. "What?"

"I slept with Zack," she repeated.

"As in Zack Creighton?"

"Yeah."

She held her breath, waiting for the fireworks, waiting for either Sam or Mari to blow up at her.

They surprised her by grinning.

"He's great in bed, ain't he?" Marilee sighed.

Hailey swallowed. "That's it? That's all you have to say? Aren't you going to yell at me or something?"

"Why would I yell?" Mari asked.

Hailey turned to Sam, who was still grinning. "What about you? No vile things to scream at me?"

Sam's pale blue eyes flickered with amusement. "Of course not."

"But you both dated him!"

"Had sex with him," Mari corrected. She swiped up the hair elastic on the coffee table and proceeded to tie her mass of curls into a low ponytail. "It's not like we had a relationship."

"Besides," Sam spoke, leaning back against the sofa cushions, "he always had a thing for you."

Huh? Where had *that* come from? As usual, her roommates were making her head spin. She'd known what she'd signed up for when she'd agreed to room with two spontaneous, high-strung models, but since the rent in Malibu was astronomical she'd figured living on the beach was worth some harmless head spinning.

The last thing she expected to hear was that Zack had the hots for her. And to hear it from two females who'd shared his bed, no less.

"He always used to ask a ton of questions about you," Mari added with a grin. "I thought it was cute."

"Who are you people?" she asked in amazement. "Shouldn't we be getting into a catfight or something? You know, take your hands off my man and all that."

Both women burst out laughing.

"Seriously," Hailey insisted. "Get mad at me."

157

"Sorry, hon," Mari chirped. "I'm not about to lose my roommate over a guy I had casual sex with."

She was either living with the most easygoing women in the world, or the sluttiest. Regardless, Hailey felt better knowing her roommates didn't hate her guts. She might not have a lot in common with Mari or Sam, but she liked them both, and she didn't want to lose their friendship over Zack Creighton.

Again she thought about his request that she go on a date with him. Though she'd been considering it before, sitting here with Mari and Sam, being reminded of the fact that they'd both slept with him, brought back a few doubts. The night he'd showed up at her place Zack said he'd had one committed relationship and that he'd been playing the field since it ended, but seriously, how big was this field? There was a difference between engaging in a few casual encounters and screwing any female who came his way. He'd been around the block way more times than she had, and she wasn't sure she believed he wanted something deeper with her.

In fact, he hadn't even *said* he wanted something deeper. All he'd asked for was a date. Just one date.

"Uh-oh," Mari said. "Why do you look so troubled?"

She hesitated for a moment, then decided to voice her thoughts. Since these women didn't seem to care about Zack one way or the other, she might as well milk them for some advice. After all, they'd been around the same block as Zack.

"I don't get the problem," Sam said when Hailey had finished. "He said he likes you."

"Yeah, but does he mean it?"

"Zack doesn't really lie," Mari mused, making a clicking noise with her tongue. "He's a pretty straightforward guy."

"Are you saying I should give him a chance?"

"It's only fair seeing as he gave *you* a chance," Sam pointed out.

"What's that supposed to mean?"

"It means you've been nothing but rude to him since the day you met him. I get that you were acting on some protective level toward Mari and me, but it wasn't necessary." Sam paused thoughtfully. "You should apologize for all the nasty things you said to him, Hails."

She couldn't help a laugh. "Who are you people?" she asked again.

Mari grinned. "See, this is why your wacko mother always warns you about wrinkles. You stress too much. Sam and I could pretend to be pissed if you want, chide you for sleeping with Zack, but what would be the point? You've got to learn to let things go."

"Zack and I have nothing in common," Hailey finally said, still trying to find reasons not to give him a chance.

"You both love your work," Sam answered.

"You both like to argue," Mari added.

Hailey shook her head. "That's hardly enough to base a relationship on."

"Sure it is. Opposites attract, remember? Look what happened the last time you went for a guy you had tons in common with," Mari reminded her. "Todd was responsible, focused, a bit uptight—same as you. And look how that turned out."

"You've got a point there," Hailey said with a sigh.

She felt something inside her caving in. Maybe it wouldn't be so bad, going out with Zack. She already knew they were capable of having some damn good sex. She knew she found him amazingly attractive and that she purred like a kitten when he held her in his arms. She knew he challenged her. Knew he pissed her off. Made her laugh. Made her feel bold and wild and not the least bit uptight.

That had to count for something, right?

ಞ෨ಞ

"Miranda, is it okay if I take a longer lunch today?" Hailey asked the next morning as she popped her head into her boss's office.

Miranda Sanders eyed her from the rim of her designer reading glasses. The modeling agent, despite the fact that she'd celebrated her fifty-eighth birthday last month, looked absolutely spectacular in her skintight Prada business suit. Her long, toned legs were resting on the desktop, feet boasting a pair of thousand-dollar heels that added three inches to her six-foot frame.

Hailey had been intimidated by the woman when she'd first started working at the Sanders Agency. Miranda had a sharp tongue and hard-as-nails demeanor, but Hailey had learned early on that if you stayed on the agent's good side, she could be a real sweetheart.

"Of course you can, honey." Miranda shot her a dry smile. "To be honest, I'm shocked you're taking a lunch at all. You've skipped your breaks all week."

She shrugged. "I work hard."

"Too hard." Miranda paused. "I hope you take that vacation time I offered you, Hailey. You need to let your hair down and have some fun every now and then."

That's what I intend to do.

She left her boss's office with a slight spring to her step. She'd already decided when she'd opened her eyes this morning that she would agree to go out with Zack. Her roommates were right when they'd urged her to do it. And Miranda had been right just now. She really did need to have some fun. She was twenty-six years old, for God's sake. Far too young to be a workaholic.

She left the building and stepped outside onto the sidewalk. The streets were bustling. Everyone was outdoors today, enjoying the warm afternoon and the un-smoggy air that was unusual for Los Angeles. Commuting to the city every day was a bitch, but to Hailey it was worth it. She loved Malibu too much to leave, even if it meant enduring the never-ending morning traffic.

Zack's studio was fairly close to the Sanders Agency—Mari had given her the address last night—so she decided to walk instead of taking her car only to pay the underground parking fee for a second time. Inhaling the warm summer air, she quickened her pace, dodging passersby as she walked toward Zack's photography studio.

She didn't even know if he would be there, but she might as well take the chance. Even if he wasn't working, she knew he lived in the loft over the studio, so there was a good possibility he'd be around.

She reached his building fifteen minutes later, panting from the brisk walk, her white shirt clinging to the sheen of sweat on her skin. If Zack wasn't home at least she'd gotten a good workout from the trek.

But he was home, she noted after spotting his black SUV parked at the curb a few feet away.

A grin tugged at her mouth as she climbed up the front steps and pushed her finger down on the intercom button next to the door. The intercom crackled, then released a loud buzzing noise indicating the front door had been opened. She reached for the knob and stepped inside, nearly gasping as a wave of heat rolled over her. The front hallway was so hot she was surprised there wasn't any steam puffing out of the walls.

To her left was a narrow staircase leading to the second floor. To the right was another door with the name of Zack's business etched on the glass. Creighton Images.

Hearing the soft sound of movement from behind the studio door, Hailey stepped toward it and knocked.

She grinned again, wondering how Zack would react when she agreed to give him that date he'd asked for. She was slightly surprised that he hadn't called her since he'd left her place Sunday night, but she figured he'd been as busy with work as she was.

She figured wrong.

The door swung open to reveal a shirtless Zack. A layer of sweat coated his broad chest and unruly strands of dark brown hair stuck to his forehead. He looked frazzled, and startled to find her at his doorstep.

"Hailey. What are you doing here?"

She edged backwards. "Um, I probably should've called. You look...busy."

"Huh? No, I'm just—"

"Zack!" a female voice rang from the interior of the studio. "Come on, let's finish!"

Hailey took another step back, a sliver of wariness climbing up her spine. Before she could comment on that sultry voice, a woman appeared behind Zack. Topless. Beads of perspiration sliding over her big, bare breasts. Her skimpy panties clinging to a pair of pale, slender thighs.

"Zack?" the woman said.

"Give me a second, Rita," he responded without turning around.

Hailey met his eyes, unable to stop a scowl from twisting her mouth. "You're such an ass," she muttered.

Then she turned on her heel and stalked away.

Chapter Seven

Zack listened to the sharp sound of Hailey's low heels clicking against the hallway floor, then winced when he heard the front door slam. Goddammit. The day from hell just refused to get any better, didn't it? First the A/C went on the fritz, then Rita showed up demanding he shoot some boudoir-type shots for her portfolio. And now Hailey knocking on his door and thinking he was fooling around behind her back.

Without bothering to put on the sticky T-shirt he'd had to remove due to the heat, he told Rita he'd be right back and took off after Hailey.

The air outside was a lot cooler than the temperature in his studio, and he inhaled deeply, needing to lower his body temperature. He glanced around the street and spotted Hailey tearing down the sidewalk. Ignoring the strange looks from a few pedestrians, he hurried after the angry redhead.

"Hailey," he called.

She ignored him and kept walking.

"Christ, Hailey, slow down." She didn't, so he jogged faster, finally catching up to her and curling his fingers over her lower arm.

She stopped, turned and glared at him. "Shouldn't you be finishing whatever you started with *Rita?*"

He sighed. "She's just a model."

"A topless one, apparently."

"She needed some tasteful nudes for her portfolio."

"I'm sure." Sarcasm oozed from her voice.

"You're being irrational."

"Really? So I didn't just walk in on you and some girl, half-naked and covered in sweat?"

"I'm half-naked *because* I'm covered in sweat," he burst out, fighting back frustration. "The air conditioning broke. In case you didn't notice, my entire studio is a sauna."

Hailey didn't respond.

"I didn't sleep with her, for God's sake. I was just taking her picture."

She crossed her arms over her breasts, causing her cleavage to swell against the neckline of her white button-down T-shirt.

"I didn't sleep with her," Zack repeated.

A moment later, Hailey released a heavy sigh. "I think I actually believe you."

Irritation prickled his skin. Her tone conveyed zero faith in him and that bugged the hell out of him. He'd always known Hailey's opinion of him was less than high, but her complete and total mistrust was ridiculous. She actually thought he would be screwing some model three days after they'd spent the weekend together? What kind of slime did she take him for?

"You know what, Hailey? Maybe you're right. Maybe we shouldn't be together." His hands curled into fists. "I don't think I want to get involved with a woman who thinks I'm some kind of manwhore." If he weren't so pissed off, he would've laughed at his use of the term manwhore.

Her throat bobbed as she swallowed. "Zack—"

"No, forget it," he cut in. "You obviously have your mind made up about me, and to be honest, I don't feel like jumping through hoops to prove to you that I'm a decent guy."

His jaw tight with anger, he turned around and marched away.

Hailey stared at Zack's retreating back, utterly stunned. Okay, so maybe he had a point. Maybe she'd overreacted, acted irrationally and accused him of screwing another woman without giving him a chance to explain.

But what did he expect? She'd known him for a year now, and in that year he'd dated both of her roommates, not to mention a half dozen other sexy models. He couldn't expect her to forget all that and just hand over her trust on a silver platter.

And yet...what had he really done for her not to trust him?

She swallowed again, the question her conscience raised making her confused. It wasn't like Zack had ever hurt her personally. They'd never been an item before this weekend, so why should she care who he'd slept with before her?

But when she'd seen that girl back at his studio, her brain had instantly roused up the image of finding Todd making out with his secretary, and the anger and bitterness had returned, and...well, she'd taken it out on Zack.

She really was an idiot.

As a wave of shame rolled over her, she headed off after Zack, wanting to slap herself for freaking out on him like that. Sam had told her Zack had given her a chance after she'd acted like a brat from the moment they met, and Hailey realized her roommate was right. Zack might be cocky, he might be a relentless flirt, but he'd always tried to remain civil toward her, no matter how catty she'd acted.

He'd given her a chance, and now she needed to give him one.

She caught up to him just as his hand gripped the knob on the front door.

"Zack, wait," she called.

He turned slowly, looking far too sexy without his shirt on, the afternoon sun making his wide chest appear more tanned and rippled.

"What is it now, Hailey?" he asked with a sigh.

"I'm sorry. I overreacted."

"No kidding."

"It's just hard for me to remember that some men can be truly decent. Especially after what happened with Todd."

Zack descended the steps and stood in front of her, his black eyes wry. "I'm not Todd."

"I know."

"And like I said before, I won't jump through hoops, Hailey."

"That's okay." She shot him a sheepish smile. "I'm willing to do the hoop jumping, if you'll let me."

"Why would you want to do that?"

"Because I like you," she admitted. "I'd like to say it was the full moon that brought on the realization, but I think I've liked you all along."

His mouth lifted in a grin. "Of course you did."

"I still think you're arrogant, though."

"Which I am."

"But I don't think you're a manwhore."

A husky laugh rolled out of his throat. "Well, that's a start."

"And if the offer still stands, I want to take you up on that date."

Still grinning, he moved closer and planted a quick kiss on her lips. "Only if it's your treat. That'll be your first hoop."

"Deal."

"And one more thing. You need to wipe away all the negative thoughts you've ever formed about me. Relationships based on negative thoughts never work out."

Her heart jumped. "Oh, so we're in a relationship now?"

"Damn right we are." He cocked his head, looking thoughtful. "I have a good feeling about us, sweetheart."

"You do?"

"Yep." Amusement danced in his eyes. "In fact, I think you're going to marry me one day."

She couldn't help a laugh. "Oh really?"

"Yep."

"Let's see how the date goes. Then we can discuss our engagement."

He returned the laugh, but there was a hint of confidence in the gruff sound. "I'm already half in love with you, Hailey. Trust me, there'll be an engagement."

As it turned out, he was right.

And exactly one year later, after Zack slipped an engagement ring on her finger and made love to her on the beach, he pressed his lips to her ear and whispered, "I told you so."

And overhead, another glowing full moon dominated the night sky. Hailey wasn't sure, but she could swear the moon winked at her.

About the Author

Elle Kennedy wrote her first romance novel when she was twelve years old—her writing has gotten a lot better since then, but her love for romance (and steamy stories!) remains the same. She resides in Toronto, Ontario and holds a B.A. in English. In her spare time, she reads, oil paints and chats with her critique partners. She is also an accomplished Battleship, Scrabble and Trivial Pursuit player.

Visit Elle at www.ellekennedy.com

Or pop over to http://sizzlingpens.blogspot.com/ and see what she's blogging about!

Look for these titles by
Elle Kennedy

Now Available:

Dance of Seduction
Heat of the Moment

Coming Soon:

Midnight Encounters

One Night on a Balcony

Samantha Lucas

Dedication

To Art and Terri, Karen and Wendy, Doug and Howard, Chariya and Nancy, Carlos and Pancho and to the summer of 1985. Thanks for the memories.

Chapter One

Naked. Sweaty. Sex.

Jill had been spending far too much time thinking about it since Cole Adams moved in across the hall, but right now she felt like the worst kind of voyeur—not that she supposed there was a good kind—as she sat in her darkened kitchen, watching through the screened back door as a nude, muscled Cole rammed his hard cock into the body of a very beautiful redhead on their shared balcony. Jill decided to call her Ginger, because it seemed wrong not to have a name for someone you'd seen without their clothes on. As Ginger ratcheted up the moans, Jill felt herself growing wet, achy and incredibly needy. These conditions were becoming a regular feature in her life.

"I wanna suck you, Cole."

Rough laughter was followed by a grunted, "By all means, sweetheart."

Jill's eyes bulged as Cole leaned back against the banister, naked and hard and in all his very large glory. She could almost taste him. She surprised herself with how very much she wanted to. Pressing herself against the door, she was careful to keep her head in shadows. Not that she thought they had enough wits left between them to look around and see her, but in a situation like this, safe was definitely better than sorry. She blinked twice. Not that she'd ever been in a situation like this

173

before, but come on, there was something to be said for common sense.

Now on her knees, Ginger clutched Cole's hips as her mouth slid over him. Cole moaned and gripped the rail with fervor. Even from her place hidden in the kitchen, Jill heard every slurp and moan as Ginger ate at him enthusiastically until Jill felt her toes curl. Every time Ginger slid her mouth off Cole, leaving his cock wet in the moonlight, Jill fought the urge to rise on tiptoes for a better look.

"Sweetheart, I'm gonna come if you don't stop."

Ginger moaned, pouted, then swallowed Cole once more.

Cole responded, voice somewhat strained, "Fine, honey, but don't blame me when this is over real quick."

"Mm-hm," Ginger murmured around Cole's shaft.

Ginger licked Cole's balls, grabbed his cock and gave it a squeeze before she stood back up. Jill felt as if she'd run ten blocks. Of course, the only reason she could think of for running ten blocks would be if she'd missed the ice-cream man and had a major craving for a fifty-fifty bar.

As she sank lower on the chipped linoleum and deeper in shadow, she kept her attention riveted on Act Two being executed right in front of her. Cole slipped his fingers deep inside Ginger, whose breath seemed to stop. Then he slowly slid the length of her body and nuzzled her mound with his mouth.

"Your goatee's scratchin' me, honey."

Cole stopped long enough to raise his gaze to hers. "That a problem for you, sweetheart?"

Ginger panted, her fingers working her clit in desperation where Cole's mouth had been. "Nu-uh."

"Didn't think so."

Jill didn't think it would be a problem either, in fact she rather liked the idea of Cole's goatee coated in her juices when he finished.

Who are you? Jill asked herself. She honestly wondered why on earth she wasn't feeling awfully ashamed of her little voyeuristic escapade. Of course, if the duo on the balcony didn't want their sex life to be a public affaire, then maybe they should have thought for a half a second before putting on a public show. She shook her head. That was hardly the point.

Ginger wrapped her leg around Cole's neck. Jill had no idea sex required a background in gymnastics. Now she was wishing she'd stuck with it, despite the pommel horse incident. She found herself mildly worried for Ginger's safety, as neither of them seemed to care that they were hanging off a balcony two stories above the ground. She also worried about the well-being of her geraniums that filled the window boxes she had attached to the balcony railing. She supposed so long as none of them fell, they'd be all right.

"Ooooh, yeah, Cole. Right there, baby."

A second later, Ginger came. Jill knew this because she started chanting, "God, Cole, I'm coming," repeatedly, as if Cole needed a play–by-play. *Okay, so why did Ginger get to come and Cole didn't?* Somehow the division of labor didn't seem exactly fair.

"Fuck me, Cole."

Jill's eyebrows rose. *Ginger's bossy.*

Unkind though it was, she took some pleasure in this. She folded her arms, then quickly became engrossed as Cole grabbed his thick hard cock, sheathed in latex. He stroked it before once again sliding it into his current girlfriend. *Painfully slow,* Jill moaned internally, but she guessed no one was asking her. She did, however, start wondering why she'd never rented a porn flick before. *Probably because watching porn alone in the dark is pathetic.* Still, suddenly the thought wasn't nearly as revolting. In fact, it bordered on fascinating. *What in God's name has come over you?*

She would have thought maybe sex deprivation, but could someone be deprived from something they'd never actually tried before? She wasn't sure—until this moment she hadn't even been sure she'd ever want to try it. The child who'd seen way too much had first turned into the adult who had no interest and now seemed to be turning into a middle-aged hoyden. Right now, with the way her body was reacting to the visual stimuli, she was thinking of sex in a whole new light.

Okay, so maybe thirty-three wasn't quite middle-aged, but it was incredibly old to still be a virgin. Unless of course you were thinking of becoming a nun. Which she wasn't.

Man, the guy's got a great ass.

She sucked in her top lip with a little too much enthusiasm and started choking on saliva she swallowed the wrong way in the process. Sinking all the way to the floor, she prayed to God they wouldn't hear her. It was early June and she often left the back door open at night to welcome the cool night air. Since it was around three in the morning—outside of an occasional cricket, grunts, groaning and sound of flesh slapping against flesh coming from her balcony—it was dead silent out there, making her choking all the more evident.

She waited, hunched in silence after the choking fit passed. Incredibly, the love duo didn't even seem to miss a beat. Ginger groaned, leaning back over the balcony rail and Jill's geraniums as Cole sucked her erect nipple into his mouth. Jill unconsciously pressed hers between thumb and forefinger and moaned without forethought. Slapping a hand over her mouth, she realized the two outside were way too wrapped up in one another to notice her and she released a sigh of relief. *Heart palpitations are the least you deserve for being a snoopy little insomniac in the first place.*

Of course, in her defense, she had been heading to the balcony she shared with Cole—who, by the way, she never even knew used it—to enjoy the spring night and the heady scent of night-blooming jasmine when she'd come across her own personal human sexuality exhibition. Although any decent person would have turned around and gone back to bed, Jill had been instantly captivated.

"Oh God, Cole. Fuck me harder."

Cole growled in response, slid his hands under Ginger's bare ass and pulled her harder against him. Jill slid her hand inside her plain cotton panties, white with a pink bow—*Yeah, yeah, like an eight-year-old. Let's not go there*—and shivered at how wet she was. Knowing it was wrong on so many levels, she still positioned herself in shadow along the kitchen wall where she could get a good view, but for the most part stay out of sight. She dipped her finger inside, spreading her juices over her labia, holding her breath, not making a sound, wondering how in the hell she could have forgotten how good this felt.

One palm flat against the white semi-gloss, the other circled, dipped and massaged until she was panting. Watching Cole's cock made her even wetter. She imagined what it might feel like if he was sliding in and out of her. This wasn't the first fantasy she'd had about her hunky neighbor since he'd moved in three months ago. Every time the man came home on his Harley Fatboy she wondered what it would feel like to have him ride *her*, to have those muscled thighs entwined with hers. Wondered how hot his mouth was, what it would feel like to have his tongue lave her nipples. *God.*

She was having positively wicked thoughts about the man. Not only had she never had these kind of thoughts about another man, she'd never had thoughts like these at all. Not once while standing at the checkout line had an article entitled "Best Sex Ever!" attracted her attention. Not once while she enjoyed a corn dog on the pier had the surfers in their wet gear—or out of it—ever appealed to her. Not once had she ever had an erotic dream. Romance novels made no sense to her, romantic movies went completely over her head—primarily because she could never suspend her personal beliefs long enough to buy into the romantic garbage the writers and directors were shoveling.

Not once. Not ever. Not until Cole Adams moved in next door. In fact, Jill had grown so content with her brokenness, she hadn't been overly worried about her lack of sexual interest in anything—until Cole.

She still didn't worry about lack of interest, though now she worried about being a perv.

"Oh God!" For a second Jill wasn't certain if that had been her or Ginger.

The moonlight spilled over Cole's shoulders spotlighting the tattoo of a leopard spanning his shoulder and upper back. She liked to watch that leopard dance and play across Cole's muscles while he worked on his bike in the street below her bedroom window, his skin beaded with sweat.

And oooh baby, the man has muscles on muscles.

Thankfully, however, he didn't look like the body builders she'd grown up around down on Venice beach, grotesquely disfigured as they all fought for the biggest pecs. *Gross.*

It seemed to her that Cole had come by all that muscle naturally. She longed to touch it, touch him, but in the three months they lived side by side she had never found the courage to even speak to the man and she didn't think it would make a very good first impression for her to say, "Hi. I'm Jill, your neighbor. Can I play with your leopard?"

Of course, getting caught watching him fuck probably wouldn't make a very good first impression, either. Somehow, though, over the past three months, she'd managed to build quite a fantasy world around Cole Adams—not that he had ever once encouraged her. He smiled politely at her when they passed one another on the stairs, but that was about it. He'd laugh himself silly if he knew she dreamt about him. If he knew she was watching him now, he'd probably be furious.

"Cole, you fuck like we're gonna die or something. It's never been like this before."

Cole, you fuck like we're gonna die or something. Jill mocked the words silently, but quickly forgot the sharp burst of jealousy as Cole moved Ginger, smashing her ass against Jill's metal screen security door. Ginger's white flesh pressed against all those little metal holes while the door damn near rattled off its hinges. Jill was so close to coming, herself, that she couldn't even laugh at the thought of Ginger walking around with little round indents on her ass.

She couldn't see Cole's cock anymore, or his ass, just a slice of muscular thigh and a hip, but the breeze picked up his aftershave. Momentarily overpowering the scent of pure, unbridled sex, a burst of spruce and musk wafted across her senses while she breathed it in with shuddering gulps. Biting her lip and holding in her groans, she dipped her finger back inside, as Cole bit down into Ginger's shoulder. Ginger yelped, then moaned. For a flash, Jill thought Cole was looking right at her, his eyes so dark they almost glowed, but then his lids closed and he rammed harder against her door. Within seconds of that, Ginger screamed. Jill made one last pass at her clit and came as Cole growled out his own completion.

Dropping her head back carelessly, she rubbed a tender spot when it hit the wall. Outside, Ginger continued to whimper and Cole gathered her up into his arms, ravaging her mouth one last time as if he'd die without her taste on his lips. Jill's heart squeezed tight. When she was a kid she'd wondered if a man could kiss like that, as if his entire world was encompassed in the mouth and body of the woman he kissed and nothing existed beyond the moment. She shuddered, remembering all the lousy kisses she'd fended off over the years. Drunk boyfriends of her sisters', mostly. She was eight the first time a guy tried to grab her and nine when she decided she'd never let a guy touch her anywhere. *Ever.*

She pulled her hand out of her panties. Lowering her big purple tee and reeling from a barrage of emotions, she decided to stay on the floor for a while. Recovering from a fairly intense orgasm while assimilating the fact that she'd spied on two people fucking on her balcony—sounds, sights, smells and all—she discovered maybe the touch of a man didn't always have to feel slimy. Maybe, if it was the right man, she'd even enjoy it.

Cole had different women in and out of his place all the time. She couldn't imagine him ever fantasizing about a woman. If he wanted one, he probably said, "Hey, baby, wanna fuck?" and she'd be all, "Oooh" and "Aaah" and "Me?" Then voila, balcony porn. More than worlds apart from where she lived. That was galaxies apart.

Slowly regaining her senses, she considered still sitting outside for a while, after they cleared out. She wasn't going to be able to sleep anyway; she knew that from experience. She was certain her geraniums would need some type of TLC after all that, and she did have a primo lounge out there. *Big enough for two, even though there's only one of me.*

She sighed. Sitting in the dark, recovering from a self-inflicted O, trying to come to grips with the fact that it was probably the only kind she'd ever have, she watched the shadow of moonlight flicker on the floor as the breeze moved the kitchen curtains, waiting for the nocturnal bangers to head back inside. She melted with relief when she finally heard a breathy, "Come to bed, Cole," only to have the knot reform in her chest when Ginger added on a purr, "Let's do it again." Cole kissed her. Jill sulked.

Once they were gone, she'd apologize to her geraniums and watch the stars for a while. What else was she going to do, go inside and masturbate again? The idea intrigued her but she shoved it aside. She was very good at shoving thoughts aside. In many ways, it was her forté.

Her gaze was focused on the hem of her tee, fingers playing along the edge, when a sound pulled her attention up to the back door. She realized belatedly it had been the sound of knuckles rapping twice on the doorframe. When she looked up she met Cole's dark eyes head on.

"Next time join us, brown eyes." His smile incinerated her. In the space of a second, he was gone. She heard his back door click shut.

"Oh, someone please fucking shoot me." Jill's head met the linoleum with a thud, her only hope, painless death before dawn.

Chapter Two

As predicted, Jill did not sleep one minute of the entire night. However, how much of that she could blame on her usual insomnia and how much was Cole Adams-induced she couldn't tell. Looking in the mirror, she added some extra blusher to her pale cheeks and extra concealer to the dark circles beneath her bloodshot eyes. Fixing the white apron over her navy skirt, she moved towards the back door with only one comforting thought—Cole Adams was as much of a night owl as she, so there was no way in hell he'd be up yet.

Even so, she didn't want to take any chances this morning, so she'd feed her birds later, water the plants at some point before they died and in general stay inside her own apartment until the memory of what she'd done faded. Ten or twenty years ought to do it.

After locking the security screen, she got down about three steps when she heard the deep, gravelly voice coming from behind her, seemingly out of thin air. As the earth started spinning too fast, she did the only intelligent thing—she gripped the banister for dear life.

"So, was it good for you, brown eyes?"

Jill figured she had a few choices here. She'd tried cowardice last night and gotten caught in the act. There was no need to be rude—she deserved that obnoxious little comment and then some. So, drawing a deep breath, she turned to face Cole like the adult she enjoyed pretending to be, only to find him stretched out on her lounger, facing away from the apartment, which was what had kept him hidden from view.

"That's mine."

She sounded like a pouty four-year-old, and the fact that Cole only smiled at her somehow made it worse. "Sorry, hon. I thought that after last night we'd moved to the furniture-sharing portion of this relationship."

"We don't have a relationship," she snapped, knowing it made her sound like a prudish schoolmarm. Rolling her eyes, she came back up the three stairs and bravely met Cole's laughing eyes.

Blue eyes that reflected the sky and the sea and... Oh shut up.

"Okay, look, what I did last night was..." she scratched her head, then shook her hands out by her hips, "...inexcusable. I have no idea what got into me, and if you want to lie in my chaise, go ahead. Now, I'm late for work." She took two steps down this time before stopping. She didn't turn around because she couldn't take another moment of looking at Cole Adams, his short blond hair bed-ruffled, his shirtless chest sunbathed and his damn hard-on tenting his work-out shorts. She squeezed her eyes tight, not believing she was actually having this conversation. "Don't have sex on it, please."

She swore to God she heard that stupid man snickering at her as she fled.

Well, what did you expect? Mere mortals can't play with the gods and expect to come out untouched. Oooh, wrong choice of words.

She stuck the keys into the Celica parked on the tree-lined street in front of the small building that housed four two-bedroom apartments. She couldn't see the side balcony from here, but somehow she still felt as if his eyes were on her. She hoped that sensation wouldn't last all day, or more than a few people were going to end up with food in their laps.

⁗⁗⁗

Cole shook the last of the salt water from his hair, remnants of his late-morning swim. He'd lived his whole life on this beach, from the time he was a kid hanging out at his grandparents' restaurant on the cove. The restaurant he now proudly owned and operated the same way his grandfather and father had before him. Normally he was out in the water by dawn. Growing up on the beach, he loved everything about it, surfing, swimming, holding a woman's hand as he walked along it. But today he couldn't resist waiting around to hassle his sassy little neighbor.

Good God, she deserved it.

When he realized she was there last night, watching him, he couldn't remember ever being more turned on in his life. It had taken every ounce of strength he had not to dump Valerie on that pretty ass of hers, grab Jill and slam her up against her kitchen wall. His cock started stiffening again. *If that keeps happening all day, I'll never get anything done.*

Cole walked along the shore to the wooden pier steps, knowing he'd find his best friend somewhere along the old wooden and concrete structure. Leaning on a side rail, he pushed his feet back into his shoes. A pair of kids on skateboards zipped by him and every breath he took now included the aroma of corn dogs and pizza as it invaded the pure scent of sea air. The carousel was busy as always as it spun around, entertaining small children and lovesick teenagers. The music from the calliope nearly drowned out that of the sideshow games, but just as Cole passed the pitch-a-ball-in-the-milk-can game, someone won big and the small crowd gathered shrieked in delight.

He caught up with Ross, halfway down the pier, sitting on a bench with his twelve-year-old daughter, who had a line in the water. He spread his hand over her thick blonde hair. Give it a couple of years and Ross was in for hell with that girl. Cole had already offered to go in halfsies with him on a chastity belt, and he'd been only half kidding.

"Shouldn't you be in school, squirt?"

It was their standard greeting as Ross was home-schooling his daughter and Cole liked to tease them about it.

"The world's my school, honey," she said, her voice a passable imitation of Cole's.

"Smart-ass."

"Better a smart-ass than a dumb-ass."

This was when Ross always jumped in with, "Watch your mouth. You're teachin' Uncle Cole bad words."

Cole sat beside Ross with an accompanying old-man grunt. Ross slapped him on the forearm. "Man, what are you now? Forty-five?"

"Ha-ha."

"So, how'd it go with Valerie?" Ross raised both brows in query. With his long dark hair blowing around his face he looked a lot like a bearded collie.

"Fine."

"Oh come on. *Details.* Do you have any idea the last time I got laid?"

"Dad!"

Ross cleared his throat, looking sheepish, "Sorry, sprite." Lowering his tone, he leaned closer to Cole. "And *that* would be why."

Cole laughed, tipping his face into the breeze, enjoying the warmth of the sun in contrast. "I'm not giving you details in front of the kid."

Ross made a disgruntled sound, folded his arms over his chest and sank down farther on the bench.

"You know, if you wanted to date, I'd take Hailey for the night."

Ross laughed so hard he nearly fell off the bench. Cole wasn't sure why, but he didn't find near as much humor in the situation, or his friend's reaction. Folding his own arms over his chest in a mirror position of Ross' sulking, he said, "What the hell's so funny?"

Ross took a minute to sober, then turned, facing Cole with a look of incredulity in his eyes. "You *are* kidding, right?"

"About what? Taking her, or wondering why you're laughing your ass off at the idea?"

"Uh...both? Come on, Cole." He slapped Cole's biceps again with the back of his hand. "This has to be a joke. First of all, you wouldn't know what to do with a kid for a whole night. Probably not even fifteen minutes, for that matter. And then there's the fact that you don't have a free night—*ever.*"

Cole continued his sulk. All of that might be true, but Ross didn't have to laugh at him. After all, he'd been being magnanimous by offering. The least Ross could have done was pretend to appreciate the gesture. The thing of it, though, was that he wasn't kidding—a night with Hailey could be fun. They could set up his telescope on the balcony and watch for constellations, make brownies or some female-type thing they sold in all-in-one sets at the store and watch PG-13 action flicks. *Oh well.* It would have been fun. Besides, how much trouble could a twelve-year-old be, anyway?

The more he thought about it, the more offended he became. He turned to face Ross on the bench. "I'm not joking." Then he yelled over his shoulder to Hailey, who was wiggling her line with not much luck. "Hey, kid, you wanna come stay with me some night?" Hailey shrugged. Cole took that positively and focused on Ross. "See?"

Ross shook his head as if confused. "See what?"

"Hailey's all hyped. So who are you gonna ask out?"

Ross choked on a laugh, got up, rubbed his palms on his denim shorts and moved to the metal railing separating the pedestrians from a long fall to the ocean below. Cole joined him and for a while the two stood there silently, watching the waves crest and roll to the shore.

"I'm not like you, Cole. I can't pick up any old woman and screw her. Even if I could, I also don't have half your charm. And where *you* are the sun-bronzed Heath Ledger type, *I* am the nerdy sidekick type. By the time I even found a woman willing to do the nasty with me, Hailey would be filling out college apps."

Cole ran a hand through his hair, drawing a breath, wondering how honest to be with his friend.

"I'd trade what you had with Hailey's mom for every one of the women I've fu..." He glanced over his shoulder. Hailey had lost interest in the fishing line and was running a radio-controlled car along the side rails. "...had sex with."

Ross snorted. Cole scowled. They hung arms over the rails, and Cole stepped up on the bottom rail as Hailey's car buzzed him. She laughed hysterically as Cole shot her a "quit it" look both of them knew he didn't mean.

"I'm serious, Ross. You had it with Shelly. What my grandparents had, what I..."

Ross's furrowed brow said that maybe he was finally taking Cole seriously. Cole squinted into the sunlight, then pulled his shades from his pocket, sliding them on more for the chickenshit factor than for the sunlight. Though he'd confessed, he didn't want to stand here and analyze it or his past mistakes in the relationship department. Three times he thought he'd found it; three times he'd gone down in flames. One of his marriages had only lasted three-and-a-half months. The last one had lasted four years, exactly three years and eleven months too long.

Even a thickheaded beach bum like him knew it was time to pack it in. Meaningless sex—like he'd been drowning himself in since the divorce was final—was all that was left for him until he got too old for even that. Because, no matter how lonely or desperate he got, he wasn't going to a cosmetic surgeon to keep himself looking twenty and plastic forever.

"Your taste in women sucks, Cole. You pick one-night-stand types and try and make it last a lifetime. It ain't gonna. Plain and simple. Shit, at your last wedding, you were both hitting on other people by the reception."

That wasn't entirely true, but close enough. His marriage to Wendy had been so bad, they'd both spent more time in other people's beds then in their own. Ross scratched his jaw and squinted, his gaze seemingly traversing the waves. A pair of sailboats raced on the horizon. The sun was sitting pretty high now and it glistened on the water, stunning in its intensity, both visually and emotionally.

"Honestly, man, I think you set yourself up. I think you pick women you know it ain't gonna last with, so when it fails, you didn't have that much at stake. If you ever did meet the right woman, I wonder if you'd take the risk and go after her."

Cole ached. That hit *way* too close to home and sounded too much like one of those women's bonding sessions. It had the hair on the back of his neck all prickly. He wished there was some way to brush off what he said with a smartass comment, but there wasn't one fitting for the occasion, so rubbing at those prickly hairs, he hedged. "Yeah. I oughta get back." He sighed, pulled the glasses from his face and met Ross' distant stare. "You're probably right, but I'm not sure what to do about it, pal." Shrugging, he slid the glasses back up and captured Hailey with the other arm, picking her off the ground and dropping a kiss to her head. "You be smart."

"I will, cause you an' Dad are gonna need me to look out for ya at the home."

Cole laughed. Hailey was one of a kind. She looked so much like her mother who was the epitome of femininity, but since Hailey'd only been three when Shelly died, she was the product of a single father who was doing his best. Cole loved her all the way to his core.

Walking away, he turned and waved back at them, a familiar punch of jealousy hitting him in the solar plexus until he had to catch his breath. The one thought foremost in his mind as his heart clenched with regret was Jill Reed, his next-door neighbor.

ॐ∞ෆ

It was nearly three in the morning before Jill pulled her little car up in front of her building. Parking was a bitch, but an extra three hundred a month to have a garage wasn't in the budget. Any residence in the beach areas of southern California had exorbitant rent, but having grown up landlocked in the Midwest, she couldn't imagine living anywhere else. After the last roommate attempt had blown sky high, Jill picked up a third job as a cocktail waitress in a club downtown. The tips from her Friday and Saturday night shifts almost doubled the rent a roommate would pay and it was worth it to have her sanity and her peace.

The only drawback was Saturday when she worked all three jobs and came home dead tired and senseless. She'd discovered the senseless part after one particular late night and a half-dozen purchases on QVC of things like waterproof slippers. Tonight, because of last night's little escapade and her lack of sleep, she was practically seeing double, yet she still wasn't sure she'd get any sleep once she actually fell into bed. Even the thought of those little miracle pills the clinic doctor had prescribed her for sleeping gave her the heebie-jeebies. She couldn't help it. Her family tree was riddled with branches addicted to one thing or another; she wasn't about to add a sleeping pill addict into the mix.

As she started up the rear stairs, she had a moment of hesitation and stood still to listen for any moaning or panting. When all she heard was crickets and the distant rolling surf, she figured the coast was clear and headed on up. There were front stairs, but they ran between the two units and left her feeling claustrophobic whenever she used them, so her usual routine was to come and go from the back. After last night, however, she decided to seriously give that some consideration.

One eye out of commission while she rubbed it, the other one not overly clear, she thought maybe she was hallucinating. Blinking a couple of times didn't make the vision go away so she had to take it seriously that her blindingly handsome neighbor was indeed still lounging on her patio furniture.

She was too freakin' tired for a conversation that would make any sense and was more than a little concerned. It would be like her to lose control of her tongue and blurt out something like, "Wanna be my first?" That was a humiliation she would *never* recover from.

Slipping quietly by, hoping he'd fallen asleep, she froze solid at the sound of his low tenor.

"Hey, brown eyes. Wanna have a drink with me?"

Chapter Three

It took Jill a minute to realize that he meant that literally. As she strained her eyes in the darkness, he appeared to only have the one longneck that he was holding out to her. Admittedly, though, she did see several empties on the floor...and one in her ficus.

"Cole, it's late and I'm beat. I'm going to bed. G'night."

She only managed a step in the direction of her door before the man's hand snaked around her wrist and he toppled her into his lap. She took a long deep breath and tried to keep her brain functioning enough to handle this properly, but before she had a chance to utter a single word in protest, his arm was around her waist and he had her settled back against his very evident erection.

"Oh my God, Cole. Are you drunk?"

He laughed derisively, his warm breath fanning her cheek when he whispered, "Not by a long shot, brown eyes."

Jill tried to wriggle out of his hold, but gasped when her movements either enlarged the thing further, or brought her in closer contact. She wasn't sure which and she didn't care. She felt like a complete dolt. If he hadn't caught her last night, he never would have wanted her, and last night she had given him a very wrong impression. It wouldn't take long to give him the right one, though. She bet when he figured her out, he'd run screaming from the room so fast, he might even leave any clothing he wasn't currently wearing behind.

"Damn it to hell, Jill. You make me hard. You make me fucking crazy with want." His tongue made a slow pass along the shell of her ear. "Do you think I don't notice you watching me? Shit, honey, I mis-wired my damn alternator last week because I was so fucking hard. Knowing you were behind me, in your bedroom. I imagined you touching yourself, but I wasn't sure—until last night."

His mouth slid over her neck, onto her shoulder, while the arm braced around her middle made a slow, hesitant move towards her breast. Jill wriggled, trying to free herself.

"Cole, I'm not who you think I am. Let me go."

"Is that what you want, brown eyes?" He brushed over her nipple, which peaked instantly. Jill found herself actually having to bite back a moan of mixed desire and need. "I've fought it for months, Jill, but all I ever do is think of you."

"What?"

"Christ, honey, what are you wearing?"

"It's my uniform," she answered blindly, still stuck on his last statement and the fact that his fingers had moved under the electric-blue spandex leotard she wore beneath a very small dancer's skirt. His thumb rubbed her flesh, his forefinger joining to gently pinch and tease her nipple, while his mouth nuzzled her neck. No matter how many times she'd had this fantasy—or a variation of it—she'd never come close to getting it right. Maybe it was the sleep deprivation, but her skin felt tingly from head to foot, her nipple ached for his mouth, her inner muscles clenched, and she found herself having to fight hard for any kind of resistance.

She had no idea what had suddenly come over Cole, other than last night. And that had been so far from her real personality that it would have been laughable if she wasn't in the man's arms at the moment. He wanted a hoyden, a woman who was brazen enough to watch a couple fucking and pleasure herself at the same time. While she had to admit that was exactly what she'd done, it hadn't been her. She'd obviously been taken over by some remnant sex spirit. Probably one left behind from one of his many...*many* girlfriends.

His entire hand flattened on her breast. *God, how I've wanted this.* It scared her how much she wanted this, wanted Cole, all of him touching her, taking off her clothes, kissing her, being the first one, the only one, to ever enter her. She wanted to feel him stretch her until he fit deep within, then she wanted to know how it felt to hold a man intimately when he came inside her.

He dipped to the side to set the beer bottle on the ground. When his hand came back, it rested on her thigh, but only for a mere second before skimming under her skirt.

"Cole, I think you have the wrong idea."

Despite her own traitorous thoughts and aghast at how thready and broken her voice was, she swallowed back the lust threatening to engulf her. She knew all about men and their desires. Even if Cole didn't freak when he found out she was a virgin, once he'd had her, he'd lose interest and she'd be forced to watch his late-night balcony exhibits, knowing what it felt like to have him in her—knowing his touch and his kiss. If she knew anything about herself, she'd also be longing for those things and knowing there would be no hope of ever having him again.

"I do *not* do one-night stands." She was beginning to sound panicked, her voice rising on each word. Although, in fairness, he had brushed against her crotch right about the time the word *stands* came out.

How in hell did he get my legs open?

She tried to close them tightly, but since Cole's hand was already between them, it did her no good. In fact, the damn man moaned.

"You're soaked, baby. Let me touch you."

"No." She shook her head furiously, but since it was resting back against his chest at the time, she wasn't sure it had the effect she meant for it to have.

"Please, baby." He wriggled against her, prodding her cleft with an erection that felt like steel. She didn't know much about a man's make-up, but she couldn't imagine that not being painful.

"I have to go inside. I have to sleep. By tomorrow you'll have moved on to someone else; you won't even care that I said no."

He cupped her mound. Her muscles clenched and she had the wildest urge to know what it would feel like to do that around him, with him embedded deep inside, their bodies entwined, sweat-sheened as they fucked each other hard.

"Cole, you make me feel things I shouldn't. You have no idea how dangerous you are to me."

With one hand enfolding her, the other squeezed and massaged her breast. His mouth constantly hovered over her neck and shoulder—his moist breath with a hint of beer on it— the rough hairs of his goatee abrading her sensitive skin in a delicious wash of sensory overload. She became lost in the rising emotions. She knew she'd never get away from him unless he let her. Unless he stopped everything and shoved her from him, she wouldn't leave—and that scared her to death. Thirty-three years she'd never let a man touch her like this, why now was this one so hard to say no to?

"I know exactly, honey. You think I haven't been fighting this from the day I moved in and saw your sweet ass out here watering your flowers? Every night in my bed, I think of you, and that's whether I've got company or not. One hint of your scent, the sound of your laughter and I'm rock hard before I can breathe. You can't have any idea how you affect me."

She laughed now, nervously. The man had one hell of a line going for him.

No wonder he scores so much.

"Cohhhle." His name became a moan, a benediction as he eased his fingers under the spandex and grazed the hot, swollen flesh of her labia.

"You're so wet, I know you want me." His fingers slipped between the folds.

Jill gasped at how good it felt, how different from her own fingers. When he circled her clit, she writhed in ecstasy, against her will. He bit her shoulder like she'd seen him do last night, and like Ginger, she yelped, but then quickly moaned as the pain became heated pleasure.

"Let me make you come. I watched you last night. I was ramming inside Valerie and all I could think about was you. How goddamn much I wanted inside *you*."

He growled and bit her again, and Jill's breath stuttered and stalled. Never in her life had she felt anything this good, but if she said yes, then what? Not that she was expecting some kind of commitment from Mr. One Nighter, but what if she couldn't handle seeing him with other women after this? And worse—what if, after a taste of sex, she decided she wanted more? What then? Did she become like her mother and sisters, whoring themselves out, pretending to be in love with every guy they brought home so it didn't seem so sleazy?

She'd sworn to herself she'd never be like them, never let men touch her, use her the way they did. She'd moved halfway across the country to be free from them—from that lifestyle—and she couldn't let it all be for nothing.

The memories gave her the strength she needed and she pulled away, but Cole's moan was too much for her and she stopped before she'd made it anywhere near freedom and sanity.

"Please, God, don't leave me like this, Jill. I realize I must seem like the letch of the free world to you, but I swear to God it's not like that. I won't take you tonight out here and forget you in the morning, I wanna make you come. I want to hear those little pants I heard last night, knowing I'm making you so hot and wet." His finger made another pass over her and Jill knew it wouldn't take much more before she came. Even now she was purposefully holding her breath against it.

He must have taken her silence as acquiescence, because suddenly she realized his finger was moving inside, sliding deep into never-before-breached territory. She nearly choked from inhaling too fast, but then the sensations took over and her brain functions all but shut down completely. She flopped back against his chest and spread her legs wider, rising up against him, silently begging for more.

"You're so freakin' tight, honey." His fingers wiggled within her. She arched against his hand and moaned at the overwhelming feelings he was stirring within. "Fuck, it makes me want inside you even more." He spread her juices from her vagina over her sensitive folds, his finger practically slipping along her skin now. His rhythm became faster and as he tipped her back in his arms, Jill was almost utterly lost to her imminent orgasm. She didn't even notice his intent until she felt the wet heat of his mouth surrounding her nipple, felt the gentle scrape of his teeth.

That was all it took. She came with an explosive quality that almost made her understand why people craved sex the way they did. She bucked hard, nearly knocking them both off the chaise, she was sure of it. White light blinded her behind her closed lids, and the tingly feeling she'd been having since he first touched her broke out into an electric frisson that left her toes numb. If her mind wasn't totally blown at this point, she most likely would have been horrified to know she might have been joining the ranks of the sexually depraved and needy.

She continued to writhe and moan as Cole moved his mouth from her breast to her lips, swallowing her cries while his tongue touched and danced with hers. Her first *real* kiss, and she was missing it. Because how could anyone think when their body was imploding on itself?

"Oh God," she whimpered against his mouth when the last of the spasms waned. Limp in his arms, she couldn't have moved if he'd shouted *fire*, and she was fairly certain her legs no longer worked, anyway. He kissed her lips, her throat, her shoulders, all the while his hand still cupped her mound protectively—as if he'd found treasure and didn't want to release it. Jill felt tears welling in her eyes and prayed they wouldn't slip free, but didn't have the emotional bandwidth left to fight them. When Cole's fingers reached up to touch her cheek, she imagined she'd lost the fight she hadn't the strength to start in the first place.

"Don't cry, sweetheart."

Never, in all her life, had she heard words spoken more tenderly than those. It made her weep all the more. She felt her lonely life with bitter acuity in that moment. She hated that she was so alone. Hated that she'd walled off all her emotions so absolutely, yet this man had gotten to them, and now she hated the fact that probably meant she'd have to start the long and painful process of shoving her needs and desires aside again.

But mostly, she hated that right now she felt like she might actually fall asleep in Cole's arms. Deep sleep, something that had been so elusive for so many years she couldn't count. She didn't want to need anyone, but as she felt consciousness slipping away, all she could think was, *Please don't leave me.*

Cole held her close while she slept, his own need still raging. He adjusted her limp body and slid his hand inside his sweatpants, fisting it around his engorged cock.

Damn, but she makes me harder than any other woman alive.

He couldn't even begin to imagine how good the sex between them would be, especially if tonight was any indication. Jill Reed was a wildfire of passion and desire, waiting to be ignited. He couldn't figure how or why she had remained single, unless of course it was some form of punishment for him from the gods. To hold out the perfect woman in front of him at a time in his life when he'd finally realized he was too defective to make the real thing work, even if it ever did come along.

He wondered about the other men in her life. Had they understood who she was, what she needed? He couldn't imagine anyone having such a responsive and sexy woman in their bed and letting her go. That, of course, was the crux of the problem for him—the "letting her go" part. He'd fought his attraction to Jill from the hour he'd moved in, knowing she was a woman not to be messed with and that all he ever seemed capable of was exactly that—messing with women.

He'd waited and watched, anticipating the boyfriend's appearance. When none had appeared, he'd—yes, he was big enough to admit it, to himself, at least—done a victory dance in his head, knowing no other man was currently touching her when he couldn't. Petty and very fourth grade, all right, but he *was* a guy, after all, and those damned primal urges always seemed to spring up when they were least useful.

He drew a deep breath, sliding his hand over his cock, remembering how wet she was, how hot. He'd nearly had his fingers scorched off when he slid under her indecent uniform, and his cock had just about exploded.

Oh God in heaven, she was damn tight.

So tight that he hadn't even tried getting two fingers inside her. He wanted to pick her up then and there and carry her to his bed, get her naked and play with her all night, but thank God he'd held on to some semblance of maturity. He had nothing to offer Jill, except maybe a couple of good nights in the sack and a divorce certificate if she was lucky. Nothing he thought she'd be too interested in.

As he breathed out his groan of completion silently so as not to wake her, his cum jettisoning over his fist, he dropped his head back against the cushioned lounge, pressed a kiss into her beautiful dark hair and let himself relax. He grabbed the lightweight blanket he'd brought out with him and covered them with it, fighting the entire time the urge to growl in her ear, *Mine.*

Chapter Four

It was the strangest thing. Jill squeezed her eyes shut tight against the sun's rays, thinking that she couldn't remember another time when her bedroom got direct sunlight. She moaned, did a little stretch and froze entirely.

Oh. My. God. She opened one eye enough to see the sunburnished form stretched out beside her. *What have I done?* Panic seared into her. *And what time is it?*

Sitting up slower than her racing heart liked, she moved stealthily so as not to wake Cole. The sun was too high for it to still be morning. *Shit!* She'd missed work. She *never* missed work. Adjusting her leotard as she stood off the chaise, she was appalled at her behavior the previous night. Late-night QVC shopping binges involving waterproof slippers had nothing on letting Cole Adams touch her so intimately.

She snuck into her apartment to call work, memories from last night washing over her with a mixture of pleasure and pain. How could she have ever allowed herself to be so stupid? All she knew for sure was that nothing would ever be the same again.

God help me.

It was probably the loss of her heat that woke him, but Cole couldn't remember ever experiencing such disappointment as he did to waking without Jill in his arms. He sat up and groaned. He was a big guy and sleeping on the little chaise lounge had wreaked havoc on his back. Not nearly as much damage as little Jill Reed was wreaking on his body and soul, however.

Or as much havoc as you could wreak on her.

Gathering his blanket and empty beer bottles, he slithered inside like the coward he was coming to know himself to be.

ℰᴑℭꜱ

For the next week, Jill avoided Cole like the plague. It wasn't all that difficult. She picked up a couple extra shifts at work, and on the rare occurrence when she thought she'd have free time when he might be home, she went to the bookstore. It was easy to lose several hours there. She hoped, given the sudden absence from his life, he would get the message that she wasn't interested and move on.

Problem was, she was more than just interested—she was rapidly becoming obsessed. She thought about him constantly, mixed up more orders in the last week than she'd done in a lifetime of waiting tables, dreamt about him whenever she slept and found herself either thinking about masturbating or doing it in every free moment.

Good Lord, she'd done it in the bathroom at work the other day.

Something was going on with her mind. It was like being on an out-of-control roller coaster and not being able to find the Emergency-stop.

All thoughts of Cole ceased suddenly as Jill pulled open her back door to find a very pretty little girl poking her finger into the pots hanging from the balcony roof.

"Hi."

Jill smiled, she couldn't help it, the young girl's own smile was infectious.

"Hello." She stepped cautiously onto the balcony. The television blasting from next door told her Cole was home and she did not want him to see her.

"So, you live here? What are these? I always forget."

Jill hadn't been around a child in more years than she could remember, well, outside the ones at the restaurant. "Uh, they're fuchsias."

The younger girl snapped her small fingers. "Right." A big smile bloomed on her face and reflected in sky-blue eyes. Jill had the petty thought that her mother must be drop-dead gorgeous and had to fight the urge to look inside Cole's open back door. She hadn't known Cole to date the motherly type before, but then, she had to remind herself she knew nothing about the man.

Your body knows him.

She groaned at the thought.

"What's wrong?"

"You want to help me feed the birds?" Jill smiled and knew not for one second had this precocious young girl missed the fact she hadn't answered. "I've got two feeders up here and there's one downstairs in the back."

"Yeah." The girl eyed her a bit hesitantly. "I'm Hailey. My dad and Cole are best buds." She tilted her blonde head a little closer and Jill leaned in as if she were about to be let in on a great secret. "They'd both be lost without me, though."

Jill held back her smile, but found herself touching the precious child's face. An overwhelming array of emotions swelled to life within her that she couldn't quite control.

"I bet they are, Hailey. Even the best men need a good woman around to keep them in line."

"So does that mean you think I'm one of the best men, Jill?"

This time she groaned internally. No way on this earth would she let that man know how he affected her, or let him know that the sound of his voice had set off butterflies, or that she felt herself growing wet already.

Damn man.

She smiled, though it pained her, and would have turned around to face him if he hadn't stepped right behind her, so close she could feel the now familiar heat of his skin burning through the back of her sundress and had to fight back a shiver.

"'Cause if that's the case, honey, why have you been avoiding me for the last week?"

He'd lowered his voice, whispering directly in her ear, but she watched Hailey's eyes go wide as if she were drawing all types of conclusions about Cole's relationship with her. For some reason, Jill felt the need to straighten her out.

Pushing away, she turned and faced him. For the first time she noticed the other man standing on the balcony with them. Somewhat shorter than Cole, the man had shaggy brown hair and big brown eyes and kind of looked like a puppy of some sort.

"That's my dad."

Hailey's voice resonated with pride and Jill felt a quick stab of jealousy. She'd always wondered how her life would have been different if she'd had a father in it. She shoved the thoughts away, realizing she was rapidly heading for an emotional meltdown and didn't need melancholy thoughts of her lost childhood in the mix.

"Are you guys *finally* ready?"

"Yeah, squirt, we're ready," Cole answered.

Jill heard keys jingling. The sound pulled her attention back to Cole, which was a big mistake because when her eyes met his, they were burning hot with desire. She felt an answering ache between her thighs.

Then he looked directly at her. "Come with us."

She shook her head slightly, not entirely sure she'd heard him. "What?"

"Come with us." This time she got the smile. And Jill was quite certain that no woman in viewing range of that smile could keep her panties dry.

"Yes! Oh *please!*" Hailey grabbed her by the hand, tugging on it in a very childlike fashion that belied the grownup façade the girl wrapped herself in. "I never get to hang out with girls and besides it would give us even numbers and then Dad and Uncle Cole can do guy stuff and we could look at dolls and oh, would you please, please, *please* go with us?"

The childlike enthusiasm was cut short by two male groans. Hailey shot them each a look that made Jill laugh softly, before Hailey's blue gaze was piercing hers again.

"You would be doing us both a favor, and the squirt's right." Cole put his hand atop Hailey's head in a way that spoke deep affection. The walls around Jill's heart cracked a little bit. "It would even out our numbers and she does rarely get to hang around with other women."

"Why is that?" Jill couldn't believe the words had popped out of her mouth. It was absolutely none of her business and she was about to retract her question when she caught the pain flashing in the eyes of the man beside her as he answered.

"Because her mom died a while ago, and I don't date much."

Hailey made a sound somewhere between a snort and a laugh. "Or *ever*. I've long since given up my hope for a little sister, but *please* come with us today."

Jill saw the same longing in Hailey's eyes that always lived in her own. Years of disappointment had buried it some, but she knew it was still there. Cole's hand brushed along the bare skin of her arm, and she broke out in goose bumps as he spoke. "Please come, we'd all enjoy your company."

"I..." She got lost for a moment in the deep blue of Cole's hungry eyes. She blinked away sensations of rampant lust. "I have to work."

"Christ, honey, don't you ever take a day off?"

"Um, no. Not really."

"Then you need one. I could let the restaurant bury me with work, but you've got to set some time aside for yourself. Besides, work is not the best way to kill oneself you know." Cole winked. "I can think of a half dozen ways to go that would be far more pleasurable. Please come with us, Jill."

Hailey began tugging on Jill's arm while Cole's thumb ran annoying little circles over the surface of her other, sending sparks of electricity dancing up her skin. Their combined pleas were becoming more then she could resist.

"Where are you guys going anyway?"

"Harbor Gardens!" Hailey added a jump of enthusiasm, a rare moment that revealed she was in fact just a child. "We usually go every week." Hailey's eyes rolled and it became quickly apparent when she spoke again that she was mocking her father. "But during summer it's too damn busy with freakin' tourists. So I only get to go once a month." She ended on a beautiful pout and Jill wondered if these two men had any idea what they were in for in a few years.

"I've never been there, but, I do have to work."

"You've never been to Harbor Gardens?" Three voices rang out in shocked disbelief as if she'd told them she'd been abducted by aliens last night instead of that she'd never been to a kids' amusement park. She pushed down a hysterical giggle and wondered how'd they'd take it if she shared she'd never had sex before either.

"Oh, that's it, honey." Hailey's dad pushed between them and wrapped his arm around Jill's waist as he began leading her towards her apartment door. "There's no way on earth I'm letting you go another day with this sort of thing hanging over your head. It's a wonder you've made it this far. Now go call your job, get your things and hurry back." He glanced at his watch. "If we aren't on the road in the next fifteen minutes, we'll miss the afternoon parade."

Hailey jumped up and down again, lower lip sucked between her teeth. "Does this mean she's going?"

It was on the tip of Jill's tongue to say no. She had work and other responsibilities, which meant she had to stay away from Cole Adams. She glanced at him from the corner of her eye. He was leaning against the railing, arms crossed over his thin T-shirt, legs sheathed in tight, worn jeans. Jill knew she didn't have to go to a kids' theme park to have her fantasies met.

Then he caught her looking at him and the desire in his eyes flared. He gave her a slow seductive smile that told her without a doubt they would be lovers. In that moment, she wondered what the point was to fight fate, so she smiled at Hailey.

"Yeah, honey, I'll go."

Jill was giddy on a mix of emotions. How could such a place have existed all along and she hadn't known about it? She'd always thought of Harbor Gardens as a place you took your kids, but it was heaven—plain and simple. She never wanted to leave.

Every sight, sound and smell seemed heightened. Every experience special. From the moment they'd walked in the main gate and seen the enormous fountain and the gardens and the...she'd been lost to the magic of the place.

"Okay." Ross dusted his fingers with a napkin, then brushed chicken breading from his beard. "It's that time again for our lovely father-daughter tradition."

Hailey jumped up and wiggled on her toes, all smiles. Ross turned his attention towards Jill.

"This is the part of the day I allow Hailey to drag me through the Beggar's Emporium and show me all the things I'm never going to buy her."

He winked and Jill saw the love for his daughter on display for the world to see. She fought back a pang of jealousy. All in all, she was having the best day of her life and had nothing to complain about. As she watched Ross and Hailey walk hand in hand away from their table on the patio, however, she allowed the words to slip her guard.

"I always wanted a dad."

"You didn't have one, sweetheart?"

She blinked, drawn from her memories and her wishes. It was so easy to get lost in fantasy in a place like this. All around them people were happy. The sounds of laughter and conversations mixed with that of faint music that came from speakers hidden in rocks and flowerbeds. The smell of fresh popcorn wafted over on a much-needed breeze which broke the stranglehold of the day's heat.

The day had been surreal, a break from reality that she'd had no idea how much she needed. And she'd let her guard down big time. Allowing Cole to take her hand casually as they walked, not tensing if he placed a hand at the base of her spine to lead her. Loving every casual brush of their bodies as they navigated the crowds.

His scent of musk and spices was forever lodged in her memories by now. His touch, the breathless dreaminess she felt whenever she caught him looking at her with guarded lust in his eyes. They all were leading to a place she refused to think overmuch on. What was the point? When Cole found out she was a virgin, he'd either bolt or he wouldn't. That was that.

Cole turned his chair and pulled it closer, tugging on hers as well until they sat so close his knees had to rest on the outside of hers. It had been a completely enjoyable day of closeness such as Jill had never before experienced. Sharing stories, memories and laughter, she'd gotten lost in the friendship of Cole and Ross and for a while had forgotten that she was the outsider here.

The brush of Cole's fingers against her hair brought her back. The lust was burning bright and unmistakable in his expression now. She swallowed.

"Where were you?"

"Lost in a memory." She shrugged. "I'm having the best day of my life. Thank you for including me."

She already felt lost in his gaze. Now, with Cole's legs pressed against her own as he stared deep into her eyes while his hand moved to cup her cheek, she felt lost in her soul, as well. How could she ever hope to hold him back after today?

"I've wanted to do this all day, brown eyes."

She melted into his kiss. She was in a place where dreams came true, and for a little while, she just wanted to lose herself to the fantasy. Why deny herself what she wanted? And the only thing she wanted was Cole Adams—all of him for as long as he'd give her.

The coarse hair of his goatee scratched against her skin, and his tongue slowly ran the seam of her lips. She opened her mouth, allowing him entrance, and shivered when his tongue finally brushed against hers.

"I want you like I've never wanted another woman, Jill. And it scares the shit out of me."

He rested his forehead against her, his fingers still holding her head in place. She felt the loss of his lips deeply as she made her own confession.

"Well, I've *never* wanted a man before, *period*. So I think I've got you beat in the terrified department."

He smiled and she *felt* his smile, an intense, unexpected sensation, to say the least.

"Sweetheart..."

"No, I'm serious." She pulled away, licking her lips in a nervous fashion. She couldn't quite bring herself to look him in the eyes, so instead she looked at the hedges, the topiary, the people, the huge freakin' castle behind his head. "You may as well know, Cole, I'm not the woman you think I am."

Her heart tore when he took her hand in his.

"And what type of woman is that, brown eyes?" He put his fingers beneath her chin, dragging her gaze back to his. "You're beautiful, sweet, sexy as sin, and watching you all day with

Hailey has made me realize whoever the bastard was that broke your heart was a fucking idiot."

As she stood there, too overwhelmed with emotions to respond, he kissed her again on the lips, his hand curving around the back of her neck, encouraging her forward.

"I'm not what you think," she whispered against his mouth, and felt his lips curve up in response.

"Then let me discover the real you for myself."

She lost whatever argument she was about to make as he deepened the kiss, his tongue no longer reserved but taking everything from her. It was the type of kiss that Jill knew kissing was made for. His hands pressed her body closer, and she was sorely tempted to just climb in his lap. Cole Adams was sex defined, and once again Jill knew she was in over her head.

"Hey!"

She felt the whack Ross gave Cole as it reverberated through his body and into hers. "This is a family park. Not a park for making families."

"Wow, Uncle Cole that was hot. Will you guys let me watch later? I've gotta learn somewhere."

Jill was mortified and knew she was blushing furiously. Cole simply stood. Since he grabbed her hand as he did, Jill felt the need to follow. "No, you can't watch, and you won't need to learn until you're at least forty. Ask me then." He turned his attention to Ross. Jill exchanged a guilty smile with Hailey, who was sporting a new hat and holding several bags. "And as for you, we'll meet up with you at the shack for fireworks."

Cole started to walk; Jill followed along behind. He didn't say a word to her while they were within earshot of Ross and Hailey. When they walked near the entrance of The Wild, Crazy, Mysterious, Adventure ride, Jill wondered if it was some kind of sign. Cartoon voices were singing from behind the rock wall, the wall Cole pushed her against right before recapturing her mouth with his own.

The torrent of passion he'd been holding back all day had apparently been unleashed. Jill's knees buckled from the assault. Real and manufactured cartoon voices and laughter and trickling water from somewhere all dissolved as her mind shut down and she became the wanton creature she'd always feared.

Her hands ran the planes of Cole's chest. She marveled at the muscles and the heat beneath his T-shirt, felt his heart beating so hard she wondered how it managed to stay inside. He wrapped his arms tight around her, pulling her body seamlessly against his. Jill felt his erection prodding her, and she wanted nothing more than to free it. She wanted to let him take her right here and now and didn't give a damn about the crowds, the kids, or getting arrested for public indecency. All she wanted was Cole Adams and in that moment, she decided she'd have him any way she could get him.

Chapter Five

"We have to get out of here." He was breathless, she felt the same. Cole took her hand, pulling her through the crowd like an expert avoiding strollers and outdoor vendors.

"Where are we going?"

"Someplace private." His voice was tense and he held her hand like it was precious treasure. She followed along without a word. She was burning up and wanted him with such ferocity it scared her. They circled around alongside a fast-food restaurant until he dragged her into the side opening of the castle. He stopped for a second, long enough to kiss her breathless again, then yanked her through the entrance and up a narrow staircase as regal-sounding music sang from secret speakers that seemed to be all around them.

It was dark and cold and he kept tugging her past windows that held dioramas depicting castles and dragons and princesses. The dolls in the windows appeared to be the only other people in there. "Why isn't anyone else here?"

He pushed her into an alcove where they would be all but invisible should anyone actually come by. "Because this exhibit is duller than bird shit and the parade's on. We'll have privacy for at least a half hour."

He kissed her again, pressing her back against the cold stone wall of the castle. It occurred to her that he sure was knowledgeable about the exact place to get privacy, but with his tongue passionately exploring her mouth and his hands wandering along the bare skin of her leg up under the skirt of her dress, she didn't care about anything else.

"I want to feel you, baby." His words were lost into her lips. "Are you wet?"

She whimpered and nodded at him the second before she felt his fingers slip beneath the elastic of her panties. She gulped in air when he pushed inside her.

"Fuck, you're tight, honey."

Jill knew she'd lost her mind. She was in a public place...*children* were around, and all she thought was how bad she wanted more than his fingers inside her.

"Cole, can't we go somewhere else? I mean, what if someone—"

He swallowed her words, sucked on her tongue and found her clit all in one smooth movement. She was soooo in over her head.

"No one's coming. If they are, we'll hear them and even then, the only way they'd see us is if they turned around and went through the exhibit backwards. This is the entrance to a storage area. No one comes through this way. I swear I wouldn't risk your safety, Jill."

Cole's hand slid down her throat to the front of her dress, his eyes latched on hers as he cupped her breast, his other hand still brushing over the heated slick folds of her labia. He wasn't sure what the hell had come over him. He hadn't been this horny since he'd been a teen, but he wanted Jill. He wanted her now. His cock bulged as he caught the scent of her arousal. He eased two fingers inside her tight passage. He nearly came when she squeezed him.

"You make me crazy, baby. I haven't felt like this in forever."

"Ah. Uh-huh."

He smiled, she was close. She tried to look at him, but her eyes closed again instantly.

"God, Cole. I'm not a slut..."

He cupped her head in his palm, pulled her against him and whispered in her ear. "Wrap your leg around me. And, honey, I never thought you were."

He kissed her. It was a deep, wet kiss, the kind you gave someone you loved, and that thought didn't even make him blink. He just kissed her. Tried to show her with his mouth how much he felt for her. This crazy passion he'd been holding back for months had swept over the top of the dam holding back his heart and there was no turning back now.

He worked the zipper on the back of her dress enough to get the material to move aside, and he sucked her hard pink nipple into his mouth even as his finger slid deeper inside her.

When she came he swallowed her screams, held her body close and let her tremble out the last of her release. She fell limp against him and he reached for his wallet to get a condom. As her head rested against his shoulder he sheathed himself, lifted her into his arms and adjusted her panties. "Wrap the other leg around me now, honey."

She did so without question. He smiled, knowing she was still lost to the afterglow, but if he didn't get inside her quick, he was going to lose himself in his jeans and that would be a little difficult to explain. He nudged her opening, reminding himself that he'd have to go slow to get inside her without hurting her.

"Cole! I can't... I mean, I haven't... I mean..."

He kissed her into silence, pushing away his own conscience as well as any hesitation she might have. "Let me love you, brown eyes." He pushed in further, but by the time he realized what he was doing it was too late; his cock had pressed past the thin barrier and Cole knew he'd fucked up big time.

Tears burning the backs of her eyelids, Jill shoved hard against his shoulders, but she was no match for the man. She wasn't going anywhere until he decided that she could. "Let me go." The teary sound of her own voice only served to undo her further, and she pushed again while Cole stood motionless with his dick inside her. This was truly the worst moment of her life.

"Precious woman. *Stop* fretting." He pressed a fierce kiss to her forehead before he let her go enough to separate their bodies. What he did with the condom she had no idea, but if he didn't let her go soon she was sure she'd never recover from this.

"We need to talk, sweetheart."

"No." She shook her head furiously. "No talking. Let me go. I'll move out and never think of this again."

He *laughed.* Had the nerve to *laugh.* He adjusted his clothing, gave her an achingly soft kiss and looked around the corner for a moment, then back. "No one's moving. We're talking. Then I'm making *that* debacle right." Jill felt another layer of humiliation descend.

She followed along like a lost puppy as he led her down a series of stairs. The magic had drained from the afternoon and by the time they reached the final staircase she thought if she ever heard any music even remotely similar to the trumpets and woodwinds sounding now, she'd throw up.

"Good God, I'm blind."

She actually snickered as he blinked and brought his free arm up to cover his eyes. They had been inside long enough to make the southern California sunshine seem all the more blinding.

He didn't wait long before moving again. She heard music in the distance and realized it was the late-afternoon parade. Glancing at her watch she saw that it was well past dinnertime and she'd spent the entire day...having fun. Until the last few minutes, that is.

As she followed along behind Cole, who seemed to be taking every back path and secret alleyway there was, it dawned on her that this was the first day in years she hadn't worked and the world was still spinning on its axis—at least, as far as she knew.

As they came into the open courtyard, Jill froze. People— accompanied by furry characters, a penguin, a bear and some sort of dog, she thought—in a small circle danced and laughed and played with a group of children. A mariachi band performed nearby, and as Jill scanned the faces of the crowd, she noticed one thing was patently obvious. People were *happy*, delighted actually. Some laughed, smiles were on all and for this one moment in time, everything seemed perfect. Jill finally saw that she'd been wasting her life with worries.

How in the world seeing such an innocent exchange could transform the person she'd been up to that point, she wasn't sure, but she felt the shift inside her. It was deep, it was real and it was permanent.

Laughter bubbled up and she released it before tenderly capturing Cole's face in her hands and kissing him. When she broke the kiss, they both smiled as his forehead rested against hers. "Cole, can we save the conversation for later tonight? Maybe after you take me home but before you show me how wonderful it can be to make love with a man. Right now, I'd like to enjoy my first day off in years and my first trip to Harbor Gardens."

She laughed again as the internal joy had become too much to push back any longer. Cole kissed her, and she tasted his passion as his tongue danced with hers.

"I think I can handle that." His mouth opened as if he were about to say more, then thought better of it. Then on a rush of air he said, "I've been divorced three times. Ross thinks it's because I pick the wrong women." He smiled and deep in his eyes she saw something spark to life, something a lot like hope. "Maybe he's right. Maybe I used to be just like that. Hopefully that's behind me now."

He squeezed her hand and led her away. The rest of the day was the best of her life. A dam had burst or the walls had imploded or something, but there was a shift in both of them. Jill no longer felt that part of Cole wanted to keep her back, warning "keep your distance". As for her, well, something had awakened in her and it left her feeling alive in a way she couldn't remember ever feeling before.

They acted like horny teenagers for the rest of the day, unable to keep their hands off one another. She'd learned about every dark corner and make-out ride in the park on a personal level. Even now, as she rested back against Cole's chest, his arms wrapped tight around her waist as they watched fireworks explode in a black velvet sky, he nuzzled her neck and she found herself reaching behind her and fondling his growing erection.

The ride home was quiet. Hailey slept in the front seat beside her dad, and Cole and Jill rode in the backseat. He had his hand up under the sweatshirt he'd bought her and—since her dress was unzipped and completely open—he had free access to her breasts. The way he kept brushing her nipple with his thumb and occasionally pinching it drove her mad with lust. Stunned by the depths of her desire, she found herself wanting Cole so desperately that she couldn't see how on earth they'd ever have any kind of conversation first. She wondered if she could unzip his pants and fondle him now in the dark without Ross knowing. Cole's repeated kisses, however, left her brain cells misfiring. She was wet with arousal and was having a very difficult time keeping any train of thought at all.

"Take tomorrow off," he whispered against her hair before he nuzzled her ear and throat. "I want to make love to you all day."

The words alone sent tingles into places she never realized could tingle. "What work?"

"Oh God, would you two knock it off. I'm getting severely nauseous up here."

Jill giggled as Cole whacked the back of Ross' head. "Get your own woman. That should cure your nausea and then we could double date." Jill's heart tripped when he looked back into her eyes. "Because I think I'm gonna do the steady thing for a while, bro. May as well join me."

He kissed her until they pulled up in front of their apartment. He kissed her up the walk to the stairs. He stopped her three separate times on the stairs to kiss her and when they got to the landing he swept her from her feet and carried her to his bed.

"I know I said we'd talk—"

This time she kissed him. "We have a long time to work out the details, just love me tonight."

He gave her the heart-stopping smile as he came down on top of her. "Oh, brown eyes, I intend to." He tugged the sweatshirt over her head. Seeing what a shambles had been made of her dress from all of his manhandling in the car made her giggle.

"Something funny, precious?"

She laughed again, but the sound quickly became a moan as his mouth covered her nipple, tugging on it gently with his teeth until she thought she'd lose her mind. She arched against his mouth, as his hand moved along her thigh up to her hip. He pulled away from her long enough to remove her panties.

"Sweetheart, I get that this is your first time and I should make it all candlelight and flowers, but fuck, honey, I want you like a crazy man. Let me make it up to you, all night, all day tomorrow, but right now…"

She pushed on his cheek until she met his eyes. "Right now, *fuck* me." She laughed as he practically tore the clothes from his body. She removed her own clothes and tried to quickly dive under the covers only to have Cole stop her. Grabbing her by the waist, he flipped her onto her back, flat on the bed.

"Oh no you don't." His lips covered hers. Her heartbeat stilled as she accepted the safety she felt in his arms. "I've lusted after that body for months, you're not going to jump under those covers and gyp me, honey."

Keeping her hands pinned to the bed beside her head, his body straddling hers, he made her captive to his every desire. When he sat up and his gaze roamed over her entire body, searing her skin with his molten desire, she felt beautiful for the first time in her entire life.

"I'm going to taste every last inch of your skin." He dropped his body back down over hers, and his tongue ran the length of her bottom lip. "I'm going to eat your pussy, honey, and I'm gonna make you scream my name."

While Jill attempted to catch her breath, Cole moved the length of her body, nipping and tasting her as he promised. When he situated himself between her legs, he looked up and met her gaze with a wicked gleam.

"Spread your legs for me, brown eyes."

A moment's hesitation washed over her. "I..."

"Spread. Your. Legs."

She swallowed hard and did as she was told.

"More."

"But, Cole..."

"More," he growled.

She complied. The first thing she felt was his fingers gliding over the slick surface of her labia, then the gentle press of his tongue. She nearly leapt off the bed. The wet, heated sensation was nothing like she ever could have imagined and when he sucked on her clit, shards of white heat shot up her thighs. Moaning, she writhed, pushing her pussy against his mouth.

Cole ate at her voraciously, never having enjoyed this particular intimacy more than he was at this very moment. Giving Jill Reed pleasure suddenly seemed like the only important job on earth. Warm summer air caressed their bodies as he brought Jill to her first climax. He knew he had only seconds before he joined her and he desperately needed to be inside her tight wet passage when he did.

Fumbling around on the floor, he found a condom and slid it on. He paused, pressing inside her nearly virgin body just a little. "This may hurt some. I'm not sure how complete of a job I did earlier. I'm sorry, brown eyes."

She nodded, not entirely coherent. "I don't care, just do it."

He thought he might die before he got fully embedded in her heat. She was so damn tight and her pussy was still convulsing slightly from her orgasm. Every pulse teased his cock to the brink. There was no barrier this time, but even fully sheathed inside her, he waited. Attempted to count to ten, got to three, and started rocking his body against hers.

"You okay?"

"Mmmmmm."

Her pussy squeezed him. She probably had no idea she'd done it, but damn it felt good. "I'm not gonna last, baby." Picking up the tempo, he tried to concentrate on remembering her body's needs. But when she started to move with him, naturally meeting his thrusts, he was done for.

Clutching her hips, he set a fierce rhythm, her pussy sliding the length of his cock. Now coated with her nectar it moved with ease in and out. Her little whimpers quickly turned to moans and then cries of passion. Each sound set Cole on the edge. Nothing or no woman had ever felt like this. He grabbed her ass, lifted it from the mattress and brought it hard against his thighs. She moaned, her head pushed back into the sheets—she was a classic erotic image. A goddess. And when he came he kept his eyes open to watch her as she experienced all this for the first time.

Depleted and exhausted, he crashed down on the bed beside her. His arm wrapped around her waist, he tugged her close and buried his nose in her hair. Never had fucking had such an emotional impact on him before. His eyes were tearing. He kissed her hard, wanting to remember it was a fuck. A rough jungle fuck.

But it wasn't.

It was very possible he'd just made love for the first time in his life and his heart would never be the same.

Jill caressed his cheek as tears rose in her eyes, feeling a bit mortified. She supposed it would be very cliché and juvenile to think she was in love because she'd had sex. After all, wasn't that what her mother and sisters did every time? Though she was no longer a virgin, she still had no intention of becoming a slut.

"I never want to leave your arms, brown eyes. I could live for eternity here." His gentle words did her in and the first tear rolled down her cheek. She nuzzled closer, as close as she could get. The windows were open and the hot muggy air sat heavy in the room. Her body was coated in a thin sheen of sweat and just sort of ached. She noticed that the scent of sex—always detested when she was a kid—suddenly seemed sexy, erotic. As her unease rose, she blurted her fear before she could stop herself. "I have baggage, Cole. Sex stuff. You may not want—"

He brushed a kiss against her lips. "Three marriages. You really want to compare baggage?"

She smiled, though she wasn't sure why. Cole left the bed for a minute. When he returned, he wrapped the sheet over their bodies and pulled her so close she knew air wouldn't have been able to pass between them. All she kept thinking was she wanted to stay there forever.

Life will figure itself out. It always does.

For now, she just wanted to enjoy Cole.

ℰℭ

The ocean waves rolled gently over the shore. All in all, it had been a perfect day. In truth, almost every day for the past eight months had been perfect. Jill startled when Cole ran up behind her and wrapped his arms around her waist, hugging her body tight against his.

"Married twenty minutes and already you're trying to ditch me." He turned her in his arms and gave her that smile that melted her insides. "I promised Dr. Hatcher I wouldn't let *this* bride get away—and at three hundred dollars a session, I intend to keep that promise."

She kissed him. It was all she ever wanted to do anymore. She could hear the music coming from the reception tent. Their wedding had been small, but Cole had made it perfect. Ross had been his best man and Hailey was thrilled at being maid of honor. Jill felt blessed; she'd not only found a man to love for all eternity but a small family all her own. She'd become very close with Hailey and the relationship had filled a longing for something that had always lived deep inside her.

"I love you, Cole. More than I ever knew possible."

The salt water rushed around their ankles as they kissed one another. Life would hold bumps, they both knew that, but somehow, what they'd found with each other, made them stronger. Jill no longer feared the future; in fact, she embraced it.

"Baby, you're the gift of a lifetime. One I didn't deserve, but goddamn if I'm not going to work the rest of my life to make sure you're not sorry. Now come dance with me."

He tugged her towards the tent, but she didn't budge. Another wave rushed around her feet, removing sand from beneath her. She shifted her balance so she wouldn't fall in and ruin a perfectly lovely dress.

"Dance with me here."

He tucked a strand of hair behind her ear and kissed the tip of her nose.

"Anything for you, precious."

As the southern California sun sank into the pacific, Mr. and Mrs. Adams shared the first moments of a life together. A life that, as it turned out, was abundantly joyful and profoundly satisfying...and it all started one night on a balcony.

About the Author

Passionate and creative to the point of insanity, Samantha lives in the mountains of southwest Virginia. A self-proclaimed hopeless romantic, she writes about what happens when that one person you can't live without walks into your life...ready or not. Her greatest joy is to finally be able to share her stories with readers and she hopes they find a place in your heart.

To learn more about Samantha, please visit www.samanthalucas.com or visit her on myspace www.myspace.com/samanthalucasromances.

Time might march on but hidden in each human are the embers of evolution that flicker to life when nature insists.

Evolution's Embers
© *2006 Mary Wine*

Earth is in trouble, flooded with pollution and uninhabitable for females, who are instead sent into space to live. As the birth rate becomes predominately male, the human race must find a way to stabilize the population. No chances will be taken on relationships doomed to failure because of personality conflicts. Males that desire a female to mate submit to intense testing and wait for a female whose results match. They will also agree to share-one female can provide children for two males and stabilizing the population must take precedence over personal choice.

Jala is an Estroko, a female gladiator who trains and competes in martial arts. Only females can be Estroko and winning freedom from matching is an Estroko's ultimate reward, but a dishonorable knee sweep ends that dream for Jala-sending her to be matched for reproduction.

She comes face to face with a pair of males who consider her their match-and their possession. Jala won't abandon her dreams because science says Cassian and Sion were meant for her. Cassian and Sion can't fathom why Jala ignores the passion igniting between them.

In an era when science controls attraction, what happens to the tender emotions that can bind more than just the body? Love doesn't show up on test pages, it flows through the blood and takes root in the heart.

Available now in ebook and print from Samhain Publishing.

Enjoy the following excerpt from Evolution's Embers...

Sion moved across the floor too confidently. Jala shifted back as she came face to face with just how much larger the man was than her. His lighter hair and eyes let him slip under her initial notice but now she tipped her head back to stare at shoulders that were twice the span of her own and packed with thick muscle. Her eyes were even with the man's collarbones and there was an insane little flutter of excitement in her belly which Jala frankly detested. A smaller male would be much easier to keep at arm's length. Sion wasn't going to be intimidated easily.

He considered her face a moment before he reached for her arm. Jala slipped back smoothly across the tile floor as his lips pressed together in a tight line. "Just because I'm a male doesn't mean we can't be friends."

His eyes didn't look friendly. Jala caught his attention moving down her length once again before he came back to her face. Sure, he wanted to get to know her which meant getting exactly what he wanted...her body.

Maybe she shouldn't let it bother her so much. It was just sex. If a child was in her future it was time to think about letting a male close enough to father one. But she couldn't divorce herself from her flesh. As her focus shifted from dealing with the pain of her injury, she suddenly began to notice her body's other needs. Her stomach growled and Sion smiled. He extended his arm towards the door.

"Maybe you'll reconsider over a meal. Cassian will be waiting for us to join him."

That flutter hit her belly once again as Jala turned to hide her annoyance. The darker-haired commander was every inch as large as Sion. There was one stark difference. Sion was willing to let her avoid him and she got the distinct impression Cassian was the type of opponent who charged in at the front of a battle.

Not that it mattered all too much. An opponent who took the time to set you up could be just as deadly. Letting her guard down with Sion could be an even bigger mistake than facing off with Cassian. Looking for a bright side took a lot of digging.

"Will there be clothing involved?" More importantly, clothing for her to wear that didn't leave her tender parts exposed? She didn't point that out because there was no reason to light a fire under Sion if she didn't need to. The man would be cranky enough when he took his erection to bed without her.

She had noticed the bulge in his pants and Jala really wished she hadn't. So what? The man had all the normal male genitalia. Just because he was prone to looking at her breasts didn't mean she needed to develop a mental idea of what he kept in his pants.

That sort of information led a girl right into trouble. Big trouble. There were fellow Estrokos who had enjoyed their military escort completely and loudly. They were the same females who tended to end up losers because they lacked concentration on the mat.

She might be matched for a solid five years but that didn't mean she had to fling every principle she had ever lived by into the forces of nature. Mother Nature was a controlling bitch who would land Jala on her back in one hour straight if she let her. The bulge in Sion's pants told her the male was interested in trying out their "natural" chemistry together.

Sion considered her for a moment before moving towards the doorway. "Yes, everything you need is waiting at our quarters."

Jala didn't snort at his words and Sion smiled at her back as she quickened her pace to get her face out of his sight. Too bad. He was sort of enjoying her stubborn streak. What an interesting turn of fate and one he laid at technology's door step. Jala wasn't boring. Sure, he had expected to want to have sex with his match but enjoying the time spent outside the sheets was a surprise.

No male really thought about their matches when they were separated. Once there were children involved, that tended to change a bit due to the care needed from both parents for growing offspring. Good teamwork skills would be essential to raising successful children. But the interaction would revolve around their children. Males and females just lived different lives. It was a fact which people in the past had deluded themselves into thinking wasn't so. It was. Everyone knew it.

But actually getting to know Jala was certainly a whole hell of a lot more interesting than his required lectures had hinted it would be.

Warning, this title contains hot and steamy sex between two and three people, explained in contemporary graphic language.

GREAT
cheap
fun

Discover eBooks!

THE FASTEST WAY TO GET THE HOTTEST NAMES

Get your favorite authors on your favorite reader, long before they're
out in print! Ebooks from Samhain go wherever you go, and work with
whatever you carry—Palm, PDF, Mobi, and more.

WWW.SAMHAINPUBLISHING.COM